"It's not nice to mock the mother of your child."

"I was teasing, not mocking."

She was falling for Tanner Bravo.

Falling for Tanner…

She was learning that what she felt for him was… more. More than just sex. More, even, than the huge reality of having his baby.

What was happening here? Crystal didn't do the forever type of commitment.

But then again, she was having a baby. That was an enormous commitment. Maybe it wasn't all that surprising that suddenly she found herself confronting the possibility of giving forever a chance.

Forever with Tanner. What next?

Love.

Could it be? Really?

They'd been so careful, all along, never to say the word. Tanner hadn't said it, even when he got after her to be open to the idea of marriage.

Love.

Having his baby. And now this…

Dear Reader,

What do you do when you're pregnant by a man you know is just not right for you?

That's Crystal Cerise's dilemma. The sexual chemistry between her and Tanner Bravo is sizzling hot—so hot that the two of them have ended up making wild love on several occasions, even though Tanner feels the same way about her as she does about him. He can't keep his hands off her. But the steady, serious-minded, both-feet-on-the-ground kind of woman he's always seen himself loving and marrying? She's not.

However, now there's a bundle of joy on the way. And as far as Tanner's concerned, all bets are off. Yes, they've agreed they're *not* made for each other. But Tanner will do all in his power to see that his child gets the family every new baby deserves. He's determined to get Crystal to give the idea of marriage a chance. And more than that, he's intent on finding out her closest-kept secret and helping her deal with the terrible heartache hidden in her past.

He'll help her face the toughest challenge. Whether Crystal wants his help or not.

Yours always,

Christine Rimmer

CHRISTINE RIMMER

HAVING TANNER BRAVO'S BABY

Silhouette

SPECIAL EDITION®

Published by Silhouette Books

America's Publisher of Contemporary Romance

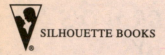

SILHOUETTE BOOKS

ISBN-13: 978-0-373-24927-5
ISBN-10:   0-373-24927-6

HAVING TANNER BRAVO'S BABY

Visit Silhouette Books at www.eHarlequin.com

Printed in U.S.A.

CHRISTINE RIMMER

came to her profession the long way around. Before settling down to write about the magic of romance, she'd been everything from an actress to a salesclerk to a waitress. Now that she's finally found work that suits her perfectly, she insists she never had a problem keeping a job—she was merely gaining life experience for her future as a novelist. Christine is grateful not only for the joy she finds in writing, but for what waits when the day's work is through: a man she loves, who loves her right back, and the privilege of watching their children grow and change day to day. She lives with her family in Oklahoma. Visit Christine at www.christinerimmer.com.

For MSR, with all my love.

Chapter One

Crystal Cerise stood in the cute little kitchen area of her one-bedroom apartment, staring out the window over the sink at an uninspired view of the parking lot. She was two months pregnant. And that evening, over dinner, she intended to break the big news to the father of her child.

The salad was made and waiting in the fridge. The main course, lasagna, was almost through baking. Its tempting smell filled the air. Crystal looked down at the open loaf of Italian bread on the counter in front of her. Ready for the garlic butter. She picked up the spreader and began slathering it on, pausing for a glance at the yard-sale kitchen clock—a red vintage treasure with big deco-style white numbers that usually made her smile. Not today, however. Today it would take a lot more than a whimsical wall clock to make Crystal smile.

6:05 p.m. Twenty-five minutes until he arrived. Oh, she did not want to do this. But putting it off would only make the job all the harder in the end. Or so she kept reminding herself....

God. Having Tanner Bravo's baby. How could she have let this happen?

The answer was simple: chemistry. She and Tanner had it bad for each other. Neither of them wanted to be driven nuts with mutual lust. They constantly agreed that they'd never do *that* again.

And then they *did* do that again. And again.

Sadly, other than between the sheets, the two of them weren't a match in any way. She knew he considered her a flake, though he never actually used the word. Uh-uh. He would talk about her "woo-woo ways" and give her a hard time for the way she'd packed up her car and moved to Sacramento on what he considered a whim.

"Better a flake," she muttered, reaching for the paprika, "than overly serious and broody and grim." She shook the paprika onto the garlic-buttered bread. And controlling. Oh, yeah. Tanner Bravo was way too controlling.

She should never have had sex with him. Not the first time. Or the second. Or the third or the fourth.

She set the can of paprika down. Hard. And stared out the window some more.

Raging lust had made her careless. And now there was a baby coming. A baby she would keep, thank you very much. Crystal may not have been practical or thrifty or all that wise. She was scared to death she'd be a terrible mother.

And yet...well, she simply could not refuse such a

huge gift of the universe. Especially not in light of what had happened when she was sixteen.

So. She would keep the baby.

Twice in the past couple of weeks, she'd tried to tell Tanner that there was going to be a baby and that she was keeping it. Both times, they'd ended up having sex. As per usual. And after the sex, well, she was so disgusted with herself for giving in to her crazy yen for him, yet again, that she never did get the words out.

Truth to tell, she *still* felt the urge to put off telling him. More than once that day, she'd found herself reaching for the phone, ready to call him and cancel this little get-together tonight. The desire to back out had been especially compelling at about two o'clock that afternoon—right after she'd quit her job. Because, please, who wants to be newly unemployed and telling a man she's pregnant, both on the same day?

Frowning, Crystal stared out the window some more—and blinked in surprise when a wiry gray head popped into view. It was Doris Krindle, who had the one-bedroom next door.

Frantically, Doris mouthed, "Nigel? Have you seen Nigel?"

"Omigod," Crystal cried in sympathetic distress. "He got out?"

Doris nodded, hard. Nigel, her enormous black-smoke Persian, was an inside cat all the way.

It was three steps from the kitchen sink to Crystal's dinky entry hall. She pulled the door wide on Doris's deeply tanned, wrinkled face and asked, "How long has he been gone?"

Doris pressed her bony hands to her chest. "Oh, I

wish I knew for sure. I went to the store. When I got back…" She shook her head so her wiry silver curls bounced. "He's terrified of being outside. Usually, when I open the door, he runs the other way. But I've looked all over the apartment. He's gone. Just…gone."

Crystal took Doris by her thin shoulders. "Stop. Take a breath. Think thoughts of peace and positive outcomes. He can't have gone far."

"Oh, I do hope you're right."

"Come on," Crystal said briskly. "We'll find him. You'll see. We'll start by going through your apartment again." She turned Doris to point her in the right direction and gave her a gentle push along the concrete walk toward her apartment door.

Tanner Bravo rolled up the windows, killed the Mustang's engine, draped a hand over the steering wheel and glared out the windshield at the white stucco wall of Crystal's apartment complex.

She'd invited him to dinner. Why?

Since they were always planning *not* to have sex again, they never did things like going on dates or sharing a meal with just the two of them, alone. They would hook up without planning to at family events: his niece DeDe's dance recitals, Sunday dinners at his sister, Kelly's….

At least once a week, it seemed, they ended up in the same room together, surrounded by family. Simple proximity—that was all it took, though in front of the others they would fake complete lack of interest in each other for all they were worth.

Even when it was time to go home, both would try their damnedest to keep up the pretense that they had no intention of getting naked and crawling all over each other the minute they were alone. They would say their goodbyes to his sister and her family and drive away in their separate cars.

And then one of them would weaken and call the other. The other, breathless, would say yes.

And after that? His place or her place, it was always the same: hot and wild and absolutely amazing.

Damned if he wasn't getting hard just thinking about it.

But an invitation to dinner at her apartment? That wasn't the way they did things. Something was up.

And what the hell was that noise? Some kind of alarm or something, coming from inside the building.

Tanner got out of the car. *Yeep, yeep, yeep, yeep…*

Sounded like a smoke alarm. It seemed to be coming from Crystal's place….

He raced the hundred yards or so along the walk to Crystal's door, the alarm growing louder with each step. When he got there, he raised his hand and knocked, yelling, "Crystal!" good and loud.

She didn't answer. But the door, not quite latched, drifted open.

Gray smoke billowed out. From inside, the smoke alarm shrieked. *Yeep, yeep, yeep, yeep…*

Tanner shouted, "Crystal, Crystal!" No answer.

Was she in there defenseless, unconscious from smoke inhalation? The thought made his heart pound the walls of his chest like a wrecking ball and his gut clench tight. "Crystal!"

Again, she didn't answer. So he pulled the top of his shirt up to cover his nose and mouth, dropped to his hands and knees to get under the worst of the smoke and crawled across the threshold, shouting her name.

Chapter Two

Nigel was nowhere to be found.

Crystal and an increasingly freaked out Doris had searched every inch of the older woman's apartment about six times. They'd checked outside in the parking lot, under all the cars. They'd closely examined the small spaces between the photinia hedges that rimmed the walkways. They'd raced down the sidewalk between the complex's buildings and scoured the central court-yard, with its swathes of emerald grass and pretty weeping willow trees. They'd even gone all the way to the rec room, and opened all the cupboards and checked under all the furniture. They'd beat the bushes around the pool area, too.

No sign of an overweight pug-nosed, long-haired cat with a smoky-black outer coat and creamy fur beneath.

Finally, they'd returned to Doris's living room, where Crystal's neighbor wrung her hands and cried, "My poor, poor baby. Where have you gone?" A tear cleared the boundary of her lower lid and tracked a shining trail down her brown, creased cheek. "Oh, Crystal. He won't last a day outdoors. I know he's got an attitude. He thinks he's king of the world. But really, he's just a fat, fuzzy sweetheart with no survival skills beyond a crabby meow when he wants his dinner...."

"He's okay, I know it," Crystal insisted for the hundredth time.

"Oh, you're a darling to say so, but—"

They both heard the low, cranky "Rrreeow?" at the same time and turned in unison to face the open arch to the entryway. Nigel sat there, his expression aloof, his fuzzy explosion of a tail lazily twitching against the floor tiles.

"Nigel!" Doris cried. She ran to him and scooped him up, gathering him close against her heart. "Where have you been? You scared us to death!"

The cat let out another grouchy meow and acquiesced to be scratched under his almost nonexistent chin.

With the back of a hand, Doris swiped tears of relief from her cheeks. She turned grateful eyes Crystal's way. "Oh, thank you, thank you."

Crystal laughed. "For what? I didn't do anything. Nigel seems to have found *himself.*"

"True, true." Doris laughed in relief and happiness. "He did, didn't he? But you were here with me while I was so afraid. I can't tell you how much that meant at a time like that."

"Well, I know you'd be there for me, too, if I needed you."

"I would. I swear it," Doris passionately declared. "Anytime." She stroked the cat's thick fur. "Oh, where *did* you get off to, you bad, bad boy?" The cat started to purr, a deep, rough sound. Doris sighed. "I suppose we'll never know…"

Now that the crisis was past, Crystal glanced at the small gold-and-ebony clock perched on a spindly side table. It was six forty-five.

"Oh, no," she muttered. "Tanner…" He was probably waiting at her door, thoroughly annoyed, wondering where the hell she'd gone off to now.

Doris frowned. "Excuse me?"

Crystal put on a smile. "Oh, nothing. Really. I invited someone over. I have to get going."

"Someone?" Doris hugged the fat cat, her still moist eyes now sparkling with interest. "A man? A date?"

"Uh, not exactly."

Still cuddling Nigel, Doris trailed her to the door. "Not exactly a man?"

Crystal laughed again. "Oh, he's a man all right. But it's not exactly a date…."

"Humph. Well. You've been here more than two months. It's about time you had a man around."

In lieu of an actual reply, Crystal made a noncommittal noise in her throat.

Doris said, "You have a lovely time, Crys. And thank you again."

"Glad to help." She pulled open the door and smelled…

"Smoke!" Doris sniffed the air. "I smell—"

"Yikes! The lasagna…" Crystal took off.

Doris called after her, "If you need me—"

"Thanks!" Crystal sent a wave back over her shoulder as she reached her own front door.

It was open. So was the kitchen window.

"Tanner?" She stepped cautiously past the threshold.

"In here." He was leaning against the counter in the kitchen area, hard arms folded over his chest. The oven door was open. And the lasagna sat on the cooktop, burned beyond recognition.

"Oh, God…" Crystal groaned.

"I got here on time."

"Oh, I'm so sorry…."

"I heard the alarm, smelled the smoke. I called your name—loud. When you didn't answer, I thought you must be passed out from smoke inhalation. But when I got in here and got the windows open…no sign of you."

She knew how his mind worked. He'd been a private detective for too long. "You probably thought I'd been kidnapped, trussed up in a burlap bag, and dragged off to who knows where, while my lasagna was left to burn."

"Something like that."

"Honestly, Tanner, I'm so, so sorry." Ugh. She was not only pregnant and unemployed with four hundred twenty-three dollars and sixteen cents in her checking account, she'd made Tanner worry for her safety. And her apartment reeked of burned lasagna. Did it get any worse than this? She met Tanner's dark, watchful eyes. Oh, yeah, it got worse. There was still the big news to break. She explained, "The neighbor's cat ran away. I went to help her find him."

He unfolded his arms and hooked his hands on the

counter behind him. Mildly, he suggested, "Next time turn off the oven first."

"Yeah. Good idea."

"Did you find the cat?"

"We did. More or less—actually, the cat found us."

"Ah," he said, meaning he didn't understand but didn't really care, either.

There was a silence. They regarded each other. As always when she looked at him, she thought of sex—of the feel of his skin beneath her hands, of the fullness and warmth of his lips on hers, of the rough scrape of his beard-shadowed cheek against her own, of the rich taste of his mouth, of the delicious, complete way he filled her, of the way he moved when he was inside her…

His dark eyes had gone black as midnight. She knew his thoughts mirrored hers. Her body yearned for him. *Ached* for him.

Three steps separated them. It would have been so easy, just to take those steps, to wrap her arms around his strong neck, to offer up her mouth to his.

She cleared her throat and tore her gaze away.

"Crystal." He said her name low and rough—but somehow gently, too.

"What?" She knew she sounded like a sulky child. And still, she didn't face him.

"Look at me."

"Right." She sucked in a slow breath and made herself do it.

"What's going on?"

I'm pregnant. It's yours, she thought, but all that came out was, "I, um…"

He waited for her to say more. When she didn't, he

shrugged, a lazy movement that made her want to touch him, to spear her fingers into his nearly black hair, and drag those amazing lips of his down onto hers. Hard.

Crystal sucked in a steadying breath and silently reminded herself that no matter how much she wanted him, they were not having sex tonight.

Finally, he spoke. "I turned on the fan that goes with the heater and AC." Now that he mentioned it, she could hear the soft drone the fan made. "And I opened all the windows." He gestured beyond the counter that marked off the kitchen, toward the living area and the wide window that looked out on the lawn and the willow trees. "It should clear out the last of the smoke in no time." An almost smile tugged at one corner of that sinfully sexy mouth of his. "It's a…real pretty view, out that window. Real nice."

She felt worse than ever. He was actually making small talk. He didn't know what was bothering her, but he sensed something was. So he was trying to put her at ease—Tanner, who had been suspicious of her from the first day they met, who guarded his heart from her as fiercely as she did hers from him. Tanner. Who *never* made small talk.

But he was now. He seemed to sense that she had something huge going on. And since his mind always went down roads of darkness and destruction, he probably imagined the worst: she'd done murder or she was dying of some incurable disease.

Please don't worry, she wanted to tell him. It's nothing as bad as all that….

But then he would demand to know what "it" was.

And she would have to tell him, It's just a baby. Your baby. That's all.

Which was fine. Perfect. Exactly why she'd asked him there that night.

Yet still, she didn't say it.

He straightened from the counter and approached her slowly, as if he feared any sudden move might make her whirl and run. When he reached her, he lifted both hands and—oh, so gently—clasped her shoulders.

Crystal melted at his touch and ordered her traitorous body not to sway toward him. "Oh, Tanner..."

He looked deep into her eyes. "Something's wrong, isn't it? I mean, *really* wrong."

"Um, well, I..."

"It's not like you to invite me over for dinner. It's not...what we do."

"I know." It wasn't fair. On top of the killer hotness thing he had going, he was being so kind. So understanding...

"So what's up?" he asked. "Come on. Tell me. If there's something I can help you with, I'm on it. You can count on me."

You can count on me....

She believed him. Tanner was like that. Often brooding and grim. Suspicious by nature and by profession. But solid in a crunch. The kind of person who would never walk away from his responsibilities.

I should just tell him. Why couldn't she just tell him? She opened her mouth to do it.

"I quit my job today." The words kind of slipped out: the *wrong* secret, revealed in place of the one he really needed to know.

He let go of her shoulders and stepped back. "That's it? That's what's wrong? You quit your job?"

"Well." She looked down and to the side and then forced herself to meet his eyes again. "It *is* bothering me."

He gave her a puzzled frown. "You need a loan, is that it?"

She drew herself up. "Me? No way. I've quit jobs before. I'll manage until I find another one. I always do."

"But that's why I'm here, right? You invited me to dinner because you wanted to tell me you quit your job?"

"Uh. Not exactly. But I did. I quit. Today. This afternoon."

He raked a hand back through his hair. She watched his bicep bulge with the movement and imagined sinking her teeth into the silky skin there—but gently. Teasingly…

"Okay," he said patiently. "Then…you're going to tell me all about it?"

"About…?"

"Why you quit."

"Long story."

"I'm listening."

Crystal needed a moment to gather some courage. "How 'bout a beer?"

"A beer." He looked at her as if she'd lost a large section of her mind.

She wiggled her fingers in the direction of the living area. "Go sit down. I'll bring it out to you. I have to put the garlic bread in the oven, anyway." Her glance fell on the blackened slab of lasagna and she muttered, "I think we're going to need lots of bread."

Those piercing eyes of his scanned her face. Finally, he grunted. "Sure. Bring me a beer." He turned toward the living area and the blue-covered futon that served as her sofa.

A few minutes later, she joined him.

He took the beer from her and set it on the coffee table without drinking from it. "Okay. Tell me. What's up with you quitting your job?"

"Nuts?" She offered the bowl she'd brought from the kitchen.

He gave her a steady, unblinking look. "No, thanks."

"Fine." She set the bowl down. "It's like this. Maybe Kelly told you. I hate my boss—I mean my *ex*-boss."

"A law firm, isn't it? You were working for Bandley and Schinker—family law, right?"

"That's right."

"They have a pretty good rep."

"They seemed okay, as law firms go. It was my boss I hated. I took the job when I first got to town."

"Yeah, I remember that."

"I hated it from the beginning. I don't think I'm really cut out to work in a law office, even one with a good reputation. But I hung in, thinking I could make it last until I found something better."

"I can see where this is going. Tell me more about the ex-boss you hate."

She blew out a breath. "My former boss is tall, blond and square-jawed. Handsome if you don't count his personality. Married. And a total weasel. He was always putting the make on me, in ways I'm sure he considered subtle. Until today. Today, he crossed the line and tried to kiss me. After I finished gagging, I told him I quit. That was it." She tried a bright smile. "Not an especially original story, huh?"

Tanner did not smile. "What's his name?"

His flat tone and the unreadable look in his eye told her way more than she wanted to know. "Uh-uh. No way. I know how you are, Tanner. And I'm grateful we've reached the point where I'm one of the people you feel responsible for. But in this case...you're not."

"You said he tried to kiss you. That's harassment. The least you can do is sue the bastard."

"Tanner. Listen."

"What?"

"I only told you all this because...well, I don't know exactly why I told you. But I do know I don't need any help with this issue. I've done what I had to do, which is to quit. I'm finished. It's over. End of story, time to move on. Are we clear on that?"

"Sure." His voice was flat, his eyes more so.

God. What had possessed her to tell him about her horny jerk of an ex-boss? She never should have told him that. Incredible, the things people say when they should be saying something else.

"I want your word," she demanded darkly. "I mean it. I don't want you to find out who my boss was. I don't want you to track him down. I don't want you do *anything*. Except listen the way you just did. That's all I want. Honestly. Just for you to listen."

"That's crap."

"No, it's not crap. It's...a woman thing. Women actually appreciate a friend who listens. For a woman, sometimes it's all she needs. Someone to listen."

He picked up his beer then and poured about half of it down his throat. She watched his Adam's apple slide as he swallowed. Then he leaned back against the futon and studied her, looking the way she imagined a hungry panther might look as he regarded his lunch.

When he didn't talk for about thirty seconds, she said, "Don't give me the Clint Eastwood routine, okay? This is *my* business, which I *shared* with you. Mine. Get it? Mine. Nod if you can hear me."

A count of ten. And at last, with obvious reluctance, he dipped his head.

She said, "I mean it, Tanner. Promise me you'll stay out of this. Stay away from my ex-boss."

"I don't like it. It's not right. That SOB was out of line. Someone has to step up and show him what's what."

"Got that. Understood. And you are not that someone. Because this is not your business. Now, give me your word you won't try to find out anything about him, won't approach him, won't contact him, won't do *anything* to him."

Just when she was certain he wouldn't agree, he said, "All right. If that's how you want it."

"It's how I want it."

"Then fine," he grumbled, looking like he wanted to break something. "You have my word."

The buzzer on the stove went off. "That's the garlic bread," she said brightly. "Let's eat."

Crystal cut the lasagna, just to see if some of it might be salvageable. It wasn't. But at least there was plenty of bread and salad.

Crystal offered Tanner wine or another beer. He chose the beer. She left the bottle of wine on the counter.

He looked at her sideways. "You're not having any?"

It was a great opening. Or at least, as good a one as she

was likely to get. She might have gently segued into how she wasn't having wine because she was having a baby....

But in the end she said only, "No, I'm not," and that was it. He didn't look at her strangely or ask if there was something she wanted to tell him. He only pulled out his chair and put his napkin across his hard thigh.

They ate. It didn't take long.

When the meal was over, he helped her to clear the table. She was bending to put the last plate in the dishwasher when he came up behind her.

Her breath tangled inside her chest, and her skin was suddenly all prickly and hot. She shut the dishwasher door. "Coffee?" she asked as she straightened up.

"No, thanks." He slid those big, warm hands of his under her arms and clasped her waist.

She stifled a silly, hungry little gasp. "I have these great cookies. Dark chocolate with white chocolate chips…"

He bent close. She felt the lovely heat of him. He was already hard. His erection brushed against the small of her back, making her yearn and melt for him.

"No cookies." He brushed her hair to the side and kissed her neck.

Oh, those lips of his…

She sighed, even though she tried not to. He ran his hands slowly along the twin outward curves of her hips. Her body went molten. What was it about those hands of his, about those lips, about the feel of his body touching hers?

Chemistry.

Oh, yeah. Chemistry. So good. So right…

"Tanner," she said on a breathy, drawn-out sigh, bringing her hand up, clasping the back of his head, pulling him closer when she should have been pushing him away. His hair was so silky, so thick. She speared her fingers into it. "Tanner…"

"Mmm…" He stuck out his tongue and licked the side of her neck. Then he nibbled where he'd licked.

She couldn't stop herself. She wiggled back against him and he groaned, pressing himself more tightly into her, letting her feel what he wanted to give her.

Oh, she was losing it. Losing it again… She groaned in arousal and frustration.

It was the third time Crystal had set herself the task of telling him, and the third time was supposed to be the charm, wasn't it? She'd sworn she would tell him this time, no matter what. And yet, here she was, her hands in his hair, her body arching, her neck stretched to the side for him, inviting him to kiss her there some more.

He trailed nipping kisses upward and then licked her earlobe.

"Oh, God," she whispered.

He made a low, masculine sound of arousal and agreement. "The feel of you," he said rough and low. "The scent of you. You drive me crazy, you know that?"

"Oh, Tanner. I know. I'm so sorry."

He made a low sound that might have been a laugh—or a groan. "Sorry, huh?"

"It's the same for me."

And then those amazing hands of his were on her shoulders. He turned her until she faced him. Her body instantly curved close to him. She lifted her mouth to his, helpless at that moment to do anything else.

He still smelled faintly of smoke from the ruined lasagna. But he also smelled…delicious. So tempting in a way she could never quite define. He smelled so very masculine. It was a clean scent. A scent that drew her, that made her yearn, made her forget all over again that he was all wrong for her.

She couldn't get enough of him; at the same time as she felt shamed deep within herself. After all, she'd sworn, she'd *vowed,* that tonight was going to be different from all the other nights.

Yet here she was, willingly wrapped in his arms. What a total fool she'd been to imagine it could go otherwise.

And then he kissed her. His mouth covered hers, and the last wispy remnants of the real world, of her obligation to tell him he would be a dad, floated away. There was nothing but the feel of him, the taste of him, the strength in those hard arms around her, the softness of that beautiful mouth as he kissed her.

It was long and deep and wet and wonderful, that kiss. Like all his kisses, starting from the first one, on a night in early March outside the dance studio where his niece, DeDe, had just finished a recital. They'd gone to his place that night.

Afterward, they'd talked about how the night had been just something that had to happen, something they needed to do, to get their yen for each other out of their systems.

Something they would never do again…

He raised his head—but only to slant it the other way and kiss her some more. She could never get enough of those kisses of his. It was probably pointless to even try.

But then he lifted his head a second time. And when he didn't immediately begin kissing her again, she let her eyelids drift open.

"Tanner?"

He was looking down at her, his eyes so dark—black as a night without stars. "When I touch you, I only want to touch you some more." His arms encircled her and his magical fingers traced erotic patterns at the base of her spine. "It's always like this. From that first day we met—the day Candy died, remember?"

Candy was his niece's dog. She'd been a sweet old mutt. "Yeah. I remember. I felt so sad about the dog. And DeDe was inconsolable. And then you came in… I wanted to jump you right there. I felt terrible about that. I mean, DeDe had just lost a pet she loved. And all I could think of was getting my hands on you. All over you."

His chuckle was low and much too sexy. "I was suspicious of you, showing up out of nowhere the way you did."

"I know."

"I also couldn't wait to touch you, to do all kinds of shocking things to you."

"It was the same for me." She ran her palm down the muscular shape of his arm. Below the sleeve of his black knit shirt, his skin was warm as living silk. She sighed at the feel of him.

His dark brows had drawn together. "But there's something on your mind tonight, isn't there?"

Her throat locked up. She gulped to clear it.

"Isn't there?" he asked again. "I mean, beyond your ass of an ex-boss who I'm not allowed to beat to a bloody pulp."

Her heart, which a minute ago had slowed to the deep, insistent rhythm his kisses inspired, was now thudding hard and hurtfully under her ribs. She had a sick, sinking feeling low in her belly. She was going to do it. Now.

She *had* to do it. Now.

"What is it? Just tell me." His voice was so soft.

And right then, before she could allow herself to back away from it again, she opened her mouth and pushed the words out.

"I'm pregnant," she said.

Chapter Three

A baby…

Tanner gazed down into Crystal's wide eyes. She had the face of an angel, he'd always thought. Never more so than now. Her cheeks had flushed pink and a few strands of her long, curly hair had gotten loose from the golden mass and coiled over her left eye. He lifted his hand to tuck them behind her ear.

She caught his wrist, her grip fierce. "It's yours," she said, hitching her delicate chin high. "It's yours and I'm keeping it."

He waited until she let go, and then he continued the action, catching the soft strands, guiding them back into place. "Okay."

Her honey-brown eyes flashed at him. "Okay? That's all? Just…okay?"

"Crystal…" He wanted to comfort her somehow, or at least to reassure her that he would be there, that she could count on him.

But before he could find the words for that, she demanded, "*Okay,* you believe it's yours—or it's *okay* with you that I keep it?"

"Look, I…"

"What?"

"Both, okay? Both."

"Both," she whispered, doubting. Defensive.

"That's right."

A silence. Her full lower lip quivered. "I…I'm sorry. Suddenly, I'm kind of being a bitch about this, for no reason I can think of."

He shrugged. "It's okay. I can take it."

"It's just…" She heaved another ragged breath. "I've been trying to tell you for two weeks now. I was beginning to think I'd never work up the nerve. And now, all of a sudden, it's out, I've said it. You know." She stared at him, as if trying to decide what to say next. And then she added, "I'm sure it's…hard to accept." Strangely, it wasn't. She added, "So, if you want a paternity test—"

"No. I don't."

She blinked. "Just like that. You believe that it's yours?"

"I do."

It was more than mere belief. Tanner *knew* the baby was his. Because he knew Crystal. Yeah, she could be irresponsible. She really ought to take life more seriously. As of today she was out of work and he doubted she had more than a few hundred dollars in the bank. She never talked about her family, about her life before she met and became friends with Tanner's brother-in-law, Mitch Valentine, down in L.A. Tanner knew she kept secrets. But she wasn't a liar. If she said the kid was his, it was.

A kid. *His* kid...

How incredible was that?

She backed up against the sink counter. "We should...sit down, don't you think? Talk about this a little?"

"Right." He headed for the futon again. Aside from the dinner table with its two mismatched chairs, it was the only place to sit in the living area. She claimed she owned real furniture—she'd just left it behind for six months when she sublet her Hollywood apartment.

She trailed after him. They sat at either end of the long, lumpy blue cushion. The day was fading and shadows filled the corners of the room. She turned on the lamp that she'd borrowed from his sister.

Then she slumped into the cushion, letting her head rest on the back of the futon, and folded her hands on her still flat stomach. "I...sheesh. I hardly know where to start."

He felt the same. But then he realized he did have a question. "Who else knows?"

It was a reasonable thing to ask. His sister, Kelly, was Crystal's best friend—and had been almost from the first day Crystal appeared at Kelly's front door looking for Mitch. Crystal considered Mitch to be the brother she'd never had; she claimed she'd packed up on the spur of the moment and moved to Sacramento because she "sensed" that Mitch needed her. So she very well might have told either of them—or both—that she was pregnant before she told Tanner.

Until then, she'd been keeping her eyes straight

ahead, in the general direction of her small TV screen, which was flanked on either side by brick and board bookcases filled with books on things like reading tarot cards, feng shui and natural healing.

But now she rolled her head his way. "No one else knows yet. Just you."

Her answer pleased him in some mysterious, deep way. "Well, okay."

That curl of hair had settled over her eye again. She reached up and swiped it aside. "You keep saying 'okay.'"

He shrugged. "It's all pretty new. You could say I'm at a loss for words."

"Oh, yeah. I hear you there." She was nodding, her irritation of a moment before gone as fast as it had appeared. "And now that you mention it, well, we *are* going to have to tell them, sooner or later...."

From the first time they ended up in bed together, Tanner and Crystal had agreed to keep this thing between them a secret. It had made perfect sense to both of them all along—after all, each time it happened was supposed to be the *last* time. And since Crystal hadn't told either Mitch or Kelly about the baby, chances were the other couple was still in the dark about the two of them.

It was just too damned weird to try to explain to the family that he and Crys didn't want to go out with each other, that they had nothing in common, didn't want to get anything started when it was so clear it was going nowhere—and yet somehow they couldn't help ending up naked together every time they saw each other.

He suggested, "Maybe we should wait until they get back from their trip to say anything about this."

"Agreed," Crystal said. "And I think I'll wait to mention losing my job, too. After all, it's their honeymoon. It's a time that's supposed to be all about *them*."

Kelly and Mitch—recently reunited after years apart—were leaving the next day for two weeks on an island paradise somewhere east of Madagascar. Though they'd tied the knot a month earlier, it had taken Kelly several weeks to clear her calendar at work for the trip. Crystal would be staying at the house while the newlyweds were gone, looking after Tanner's niece, DeDe. Tanner, whose job often took him away from Sacramento for days at a time, was supposed to be helping out Crystal whenever his schedule allowed.

Crystal stared glumly at the dark TV again. "Strange. For two weeks, all I've thought about is how I had to tell you. And now that I have, I feel…I don't know. Limp. Numb. Like I don't know what to do next."

"It's—" he almost said *okay,* but stopped himself just in time "—all right."

She looked at him, forced a smile. "Just think. If I'd only kept my mouth shut, we could be having great sex right now, instead of sitting here on this futon not knowing what to say to each other."

"I'm glad you told me," he said gruffly.

Another silence fell between them. He heard her sigh. She stared across the room again as he considered the question of what to do next.

To Tanner, family was everything. And now this woman was having his baby. She wasn't the woman he'd planned to settle down with. Whenever he thought of getting serious with a woman, which he'd always imagined would happen eventually, he'd pictured a quiet, steady kind of person at his side, a practical, thrifty woman—in short, a woman nothing like the one slumped next to him on the futon now.

Then again, he *was* thirty-one, and where was this ideal woman he'd always told himself he was looking for? Now and then over the years, he'd met women like the one he'd always told himself he wanted. He'd asked each of those admirable females out. They'd all bored him silly.

Crystal never bored him. Also, she was already more or less a part of his family. Not to mention the only woman he'd had on his mind—or in his bed—since she came rolling into town in that dusty red Camaro of hers two and a half months ago.

Most important, he had to think of the baby's welfare. Yeah, he wanted his kid to have his name. What man wouldn't want that? But even more than his name, Tanner wanted him to grow up in a real family, the kind he'd never had as a kid.

Crystal heaved a sigh. "Oh, well. It had to be done. You needed to know. And I'm glad I've finally told you."

He stared at her profile, thinking that even in ripped-out jeans and a red-and-white striped T-shirt she looked like a princess in some old-timey fairy tale. Her features were even and delicate, her skin that classic peaches and cream. And then there was all that gorgeous, curly hair. He liked to bury his face in it when they were making love, to wrap it around his fist....

She rolled her head his way again. "And one thing I really do want to make clear to you—I mean, I know how you are...."

He gave her the lifted eyebrow. "Oh, yeah? How's that?"

"You're a total traditionalist at heart."

He already knew he wasn't going to like whatever was coming next. "So what if I am?"

She reached across and put her hand on his arm, as if to steady him for what she was going to say next. And then she laid it on him. "I need you to understand, right now from the first, that marriage is not on the agenda."

Should he have known that was coming? Probably. He lowered his arm out from under her touch. "So there's an agenda, huh?"

"It's only a figure of speech—meaning 'in the plan.' Marriage is not in the plan. I want us to learn to work together to make the best life we can for the baby. I'm hoping that over the months and years to come our…connection as single parents will evolve."

Evolve? She wanted them to *evolve?* Like something that crawled up out of the ocean and eventually learned to stand on two legs? Though he had a fine poker face and used it at that moment, it irked him no end that she said 'in the plan,' as if there was only one plan—*the* plan, meaning *her* plan.

However, it was enough for the moment that she'd gotten the truth out of that beautiful mouth of hers. There would be plenty of time later to discuss the marriage issue. For now he said, in the same neutral tone he'd been using most of the evening, "Well, all right."

"Great." She straightened up and gave him a bright smile and a brisk nod, as if their single-parent future was all settled.

It wasn't. Not by a long shot. True, the two of them were no match made in heaven. But still, maybe the marriage angle deserved at least a *little* consideration….

* * *

The shining black limousine was waiting at the curb in front of Kelly's house when Crystal arrived the next morning at ten. The windows of the big car were tinted, so she couldn't see the driver, but she knew there was one in there.

Mitch, an entrepreneur who owned companies in Dallas and in L.A., must have ordered the car to drive him and Kelly to the airport. He often used limos to get around, so the sight of it was no surprise.

Tanner's car was there, too, parked in the driveway. Not surprising, either. Of course, he'd want to be there to wish the newlyweds a great trip.

Crystal pulled in next to the black Mustang. He'd been so great about everything last night, so gentle and sweet and accepting. And so agreeable, too.

Agreeable. She smiled to herself. It wasn't a word she would have associated with the tall, dark and devastatingly sexy Tanner—until now. How wrong she had been.

She got out of the car and strolled up the front walk, enjoying the bright May sunshine, so warm on her back, admiring the red roses in bloom near the porch. Such a fine, fine day. And her life seemed to be shaping up. No, she didn't have a job. But she would find one, soon. And Tanner knew about the baby.

Things could be worse.

Then a harried-looking Kelly pulled open the front door. "You're here. Good." Her smooth brows were drawn together in a distracted-looking frown.

"What's going on?" Crystal stepped up into the entry hall.

"It's DeDe." Kelly shook her head. Deirdre was

Mitch's natural child, the result of his and Kelly's high school love affair. But when Kelly had left town to live with her newfound brother, Mitch had broken off their relationship and disappeared—after which Kelly had discovered she was having his baby.

Ten years had passed before Kelly had found him again. Now Kelly had the man she'd never stopped loving. Mitch had the family he needed more than anything. And DeDe had her father, at last. Everything should have been perfect.

Kelly added softly, "She used to be the most level-headed, easygoing kid around. But sometimes lately, I just don't know…."

"Where is she?"

"In her room. Throwing one hell of a tantrum. Mitch is in there with her. She's decided she doesn't want us to go."

Crystal made a low, sympathetic noise.

Kelly gestured toward the living room, and the kitchen beyond. "Tanner's here." All the old fondness was back in her voice when Kelly said her brother's name. Something had gone wrong between Tanner and Kelly when Mitch had come back. Neither of them would talk about it. But whatever the problem was, it seemed to be over now. "Give us a minute or two. We're trying to settle her down before we go."

"Courage."

"Thanks. I'll need it." Kelly disappeared down the hall.

Dropping her purse on the low bench by the big bay window as she passed, Crystal went through the living room. In the kitchen, she found Tanner sitting at the table with a full mug of coffee in front of him.

"'Morning," he said, his deep voice sending the inevitable thrill coursing through her.

"Hi." She pulled out a chair.

"There's coffee…" He frowned. "Or is that off the menu now?"

"Pretty much. Not that I mind. I was never real big on coffee, anyway. Kelly's got some herbal teas—but maybe later." His hair was still damp from his morning shower. She wanted to touch it, to put her hand on the side of his freshly shaved cheek—but no. Kelly or Mitch might come in any minute. And they were keeping their relationship to themselves until after the honeymoon.

Their relationship. Crystal almost smiled. Now, with the baby coming and his easy acceptance of the fact, it seemed okay to call this thing between them a relationship. True, it wasn't your usual kind of relationship. They weren't headed for a lifetime of love and marriage or anything. But they were committed to the baby, and they were going to work together to be good parents. Now, by any definition of the word, they had a relationship. An important one.

And she found that it pleased her, to think of the two of them as more than just matching sets of wild hormones unable to keep from jumping each other at every possible opportunity.

"What's up with DeDe?" She kept her voice low.

"Acting out," he spoke out of the corner of his mouth. "Big time."

"Should we do something, you think? I'd hate to see them postpone their trip."

"Do something like what?"

She thought about that and shrugged. "Good question."

"Don't worry. They're not backing out of the trip. Or so they said a few minutes ago…."

Right then they heard a door open in the hallway, then Mitch's voice: "Come on, Kell. We have to get going…."

A cry—from DeDe. "Oh, Dad. How can you do this? How can you just go?"

"Stop it," said Kelly. "Stop it now."

"But—"

"Enough." Kelly's voice was flat and final. "Your father and I are going on our honeymoon and your behaving badly is not going to stop us."

DeDe muttered something that Crystal couldn't make out.

Then Kelly spoke again, in a tone that would tolerate no argument. "Wipe your eyes and blow your nose. And come out and say goodbye to us. Now."

Footsteps in the hallway. Kelly and Mitch came in through the dining room, looking stressed out when they should have been happy and dewy-eyed, a pair of newlyweds heading off for two weeks of romance in a tropical paradise.

Crystal rose as they entered. She went and hugged them both, Kelly first. When she got to Mitch, she said, "Please don't worry about DeDe. As soon as you're gone, she'll snap out of it, I'm sure."

Mitch's brown eyes were full of doubts. "Hold that thought. Because we *are* going and that's that. The limo's packed up and we're outta here." He took Crystal's hand and pressed a check into it.

She looked down at it and shook her head. "It's way too much. Food is only going to be—"

"Crys." Kelly stepped in. "We want to be sure that everything's handled. Extra is better than not enough."

"Yeah," Mitch added dryly. "Take the money. For

once." He was always trying to give her money—like the honorary big brother he was to her. He had a fortune and somehow she was always just barely scraping by. He never understood that it was a point of pride with her to pay her own way.

"Thanks," she said, accepting that now wasn't the time to argue about it.

Tanner said, "Don't worry. We'll take care of DeDe. She'll be fine."

We? DeDe's care, after all, was to be mostly on Crystal. Tanner would be around when he could manage it. She sent him a questioning glance and he gave her a nod. Whatever *that* meant.

Then again, he would want them to know he had her back. She was glad for that. Truly.

More footsteps in the hall. DeDe appeared, followed by the scruffy brown dog she'd named Cisco, a stray Mitch had found and adopted after the loss of Candy. The dog dropped to its haunches and panted in contentment.

DeDe, on the other hand, had a red nose and a look of pure misery in her puffy eyes. She wore a purple leotard and tights to match.

"Goodbye," she said glumly and held up her cheek to be kissed.

Mitch and Kelly exchanged bleak glances. But neither wavered. They hugged their daughter and told her they loved her. DeDe bore their attention with the brave determination of a tragic heroine condemned to a horrible and hopeless fate.

Kelly pointed out the calendar she'd made of DeDe's numerous activities. It was mounted by magnet on the fridge, a list of phone numbers beside it. "Cell phone service will be undependable. But there are landlines in the suite. And if you call the resort's main desk, they'll track us down. So you can always reach us," she said. "Anytime."

Tanner stood. "We're on it." There was that *we* again. "Don't worry."

Kelly grabbed him in a hug. "I just want to be sure we've covered everything. You both already have keys...."

"It's going to be fine," Crystal promised.

They all moved toward the front door—even the sulking DeDe, who trailed behind the others, still angry but unwilling to let her parents go without giving them a final, reluctant wave goodbye. The dog followed DeDe, taking up the rear.

The four of them—Crystal, Tanner, DeDe and Cisco—stood out on the sidewalk until the limo rounded the corner. DeDe turned for the house first.

Inside, the nine-year-old went straight to her room, the faithful mutt at her heels.

Crystal started to follow, but Tanner caught her hand. He shook his head and said low, "Don't get all over her now. Let her settle down a little."

Crystal decided he was probably right. "Good point." She pulled her hand free. It felt much too good tucked so warmly in his.

"She's leaving in a few minutes anyway," he said. "Some lesson or other, I think."

Crystal went into the kitchen to double-check the calendar. Sure enough, a lesson at eleven and an afternoon at a friend's to follow.

Tanner stuck his head in the doorway from the living room. "Am I right?"

"Yep."

DeDe, wearing her purple backpack, trudged back in from the hallway. "I have to go now," she said loftily. "I have modern dance at eleven. Mrs. Lu is picking me up. Then we'll go to Mia's after." Mia Lu was in several of DeDe's dance classes as well as in her class at school. The two girls were good friends. "I'll be back by four. If that's okay."

Crystal gave her a smile. "See you at four, then."

DeDe sniffed, a sound that was followed by a heavy sigh. "Well. Okay, then. Bye…"

Tanner nodded. "Later."

"Cisco. Stay," DeDe commanded. The dog gave a low whine and sat. DeDe went out the front door. By silent agreement, Crystal and Tanner moved to the bay window in the living room. They watched as Mrs. Lu drove up in her white van. DeDe got in and the van drove away.

Tanner grunted. "That kid. She used to be so reasonable." He nudged her gently with his elbow. "Maybe you should chant to make her change her attitude."

"Ha-ha."

"Or maybe she needs a hot rock massage…."

She granted him a glance of cool superiority. "How many times do I have to explain to you that enlightenment is a personal journey? She has to *want* to change. That's the first, all-important step."

"Woo-woo," he said.

"Tease me all you want, but deep down, you know what I'm saying is true."

He put his arm around her, a fond sort of gesture, as they stood there gazing out the window together. She didn't pull away. It felt good—companionable.

And he said in a musing tone, "Even as a baby, she would lie there making happy, cooing sounds. Hardly ever cried. I gotta say, the way she's been behaving lately, I almost wish she was a baby again. I'll take the loaded diapers and the feedings every four hours, any day."

That's right, Crystal thought. Kelly was still in high school when she had DeDe—and living with her big brother at the time. Tanner would know all about DeDe as a baby. The idea pleased her. He might be a tough, private eye type, but he did have experience with babies. More experience than she had, when you came right down to it.

She predicted, "I'm sure DeDe'll get used to the changes having her dad around has made in her life. She'll be her old self again in time, just watch."

Tanner grunted. "I only hope it's soon. Think. She's almost ten. She'll be a teenager before you know it. When that happens, all bets are off."

Crystal's thoughts strayed back to the baby—*their* baby. "It's not easy, is it, raising a child?"

He put on a dark look. "Hell, no." And then he grinned. "Haven't you heard? Only crazy people have kids."

She laughed. "Crazy. Right."

"That's us," he said low. "Out of our minds in a big, big way." And they shared a long look of what could only be called mutual understanding. Bizarre. Crystal and Tanner, all bondy together. But then he said, "Well, I guess we ought to bring our stuff in, get settled, all that…." He dropped his arm from around her shoulders and started for the door.

Our stuff? The good feeling fled. He *was* up to something.

"Wait a minute."

He turned back to her. "Yeah?"

"You just said *our* stuff?"

"That's right." His expression was way too innocuous—and Tanner Bravo was *never* innocuous. The vague sense of alarm she felt ratcheted up a notch. Then he said, "I gave it some thought last night after I left your place, and I realized that this was a great opportunity and we shouldn't let it pass us by."

She stared at him, not following. "A great opportunity?"

"Oh, yeah."

"For what?"

"To live together."

She still didn't understand. "But…why would we want to live together?"

"Oh, come on, Crys. You know it's a good idea."

"No. No, I don't. There's no reason we need to share a house."

"Yeah. We do."

"No. We don't."

"Think of it this way. It's like an experiment. To see how we get along, being around each other every day. Just in case."

She fell back a step. "Just in case…what?"

"In case we decide we want to get married, after all."

Chapter Four

Tanner wanted to grab her and kiss her. He'd been wanting to take her in his arms since the moment she'd walked into the kitchen, before Kelly and Mitch had taken off.

But judging by the look on her face when he'd said the word *married,* kisses were not in the offing.

She said, so carefully, "Tanner. I thought I explained to you. There's not going to be any marriage."

"Yeah." He gave her a thoughtful nod. "You explained that."

Her cheeks were flushed. A pulse beat in the curve of her throat. Total frustration. It came off her in waves. "And...we agreed about not getting married. You said okay."

"Okay can mean a whole lot of things, Crystal. For

instance, 'Okay, I hear you.' And I did. I heard you. Doesn't mean I agreed with you."

She folded her arms around herself. Tight. "I'm not going to marry you. That's that. You'd better get used to it."

He could have gotten irritated. But no. He'd thought this whole thing through. Any show of anger on his part would only make her more determined to resist him.

So he asked in a lazy, good-natured tone, "I've been wondering. What have you got against marriage?"

"Nothing," she answered, too quickly. Then she qualified her statement. "I mean, you know. In principle."

"You have nothing against marriage, in principle…."

"Isn't that what I said?"

"Only in reality?"

"No. That's not what I meant. I meant that I think marriage is great as an institution. I have nothing but admiration for couples who love each other and want to work together to build a life and all that. I just don't think you and I are cut out for it. At least not with each other."

"Why not give us a chance? We might surprise you."

She made a scoffing sound. "Oh, I doubt that."

"Hey, don't be so rigid."

She stiffened where she stood. "I am not rigid."

Tanner hid a grin. That one must have stung. Crystal prided herself on going with the flow and all that crap. She was the ultimate play-it-as-it-lays kind of woman. Calling her rigid had gotten her right where she lived. Which was what he'd intended.

He said gently, "Yeah. You are. You're being rigid. And that's not like you. You could…give it a chance, couldn't you? Kind of…roll with the punches."

She looked at him sideways. "*You're* telling *me* to roll with the punches?"

"Wild, huh?"

"Well, and what do you mean, give it a chance? I don't see marriage as something you…take a chance at. Like the lottery or the slot machines in Vegas. When and if I ever get married, I want to be sure I'm making the right decision. I want my marriage to last."

Patiently, he explained himself. "I meant give the *idea* of you and me getting married a chance. Think about it. That's all."

She glanced away. He knew then that he was making progress. A moment later, she huffed out a breath. "I just don't…last night, you didn't even hint that you might be considering marriage."

He reached out, pried her top hand free where she had clutched it around herself and cradled it in both of his. "Be fair. You've known about the baby for weeks. You've had all that time to think about what you wanted to do."

Now she looked at him. Finally. A look of indecision, which was good. Excellent, even. "Well, yes," she said. "I understand. Of course you need time…"

"Come on. Come here…" He pulled her to the couch and guided her down next to him. Then he said, using words she might have chosen herself, "I only want you to be…open to all the possibilities, that's all."

She cleared her throat. "Well, of course I'm open. But I don't want to get marr—"

"Shh." He touched her mouth, lightly. "Listen."

"What?"

"I've made some calls. Got a couple of colleagues to take over the trips I had scheduled in the next two weeks—everything else I have working, the things I need to handle myself…they're all right here in town, or within a fifty mile radius, anyway. And that means I can help you out with DeDe. I can stay here."

"I don't need for you to stay here."

He let a moment of silence elapse before asking, "What are you so afraid of, Crystal?"

She pinched up her mouth at him. "I'm not afraid of anything."

"I think you are. You're afraid of marriage. And you're afraid of me."

"No. No, I'm not. I…I respect the institution of marriage. Someday, I might even get married myself. To the right kind of guy."

"Which I'm not?" Okay. Now he was starting to get a little ticked off at her.

"No," she said defiantly. "You're not. Not for me— a fact which you know, as we've both agreed every time we had sex together that it was never going to go anywhere because we weren't suited to each other, which is why we were never going to have sex again."

"And then we did."

"Not the point."

"True." He chose his next words with great care. "I just want you to realize that everything's changed now that you're pregnant."

"But I do realize that."

"Good. Now, all our past agreements about how we weren't going to be together are just that. Gone. Done. Over. Now, I think we have a responsibility to see if, just maybe, we might be able to get it together for a lifetime, after all."

That shut her up. For maybe five seconds. And when she did speak, she conceded. Sort of. "I…all right. I see your point. You never know. Anything's possible and we should be open. We shouldn't close off any avenue out of hand."

"Good." He rose. "Then it's settled. I'll stay."

She gazed up at him, looking adorably puzzled. "Since when was that settled?"

"Since we decided that we've got a built-in opportunity here, to give living together a try, an opportunity we both agree we shouldn't pass up."

"I don't remember agreeing to that—I mean, not exactly."

"Come on, Crystal. Stop waffling and give us both a break here."

"I just…" And then she sighed. "It's not as if I can stop you from staying here if you're going to insist."

"You're right. You can't. And I am."

"But…"

"What?"

"Well, just for the sake of clarity. I get the guest room and we are not sleeping in the same bed. DeDe doesn't need that. She's confused enough already."

Damn. He'd been looking forward to whole nights in bed with her for a change. But she had a point about DeDe.

Then again, his niece was gone a lot. She took a boatload of different dance lessons, and she had a whole bunch of friends. There was always a sleepover at somebody's house. He and Crystal would have plenty of time alone, just the two of them….

"Fine," he said, trying to look agreeable and harmless, which they both knew he wasn't. "It won't be the first time I've slept on the daybed in Kelly's office."

She frowned and he knew she was feeling guilty for taking the better bedroom. "You could use Mitch and Kelly's room…."

"Naw. The daybed will do fine." He held down a hand to her. "So what do you say? Let's bring our stuff in."

She looked at him sideways for a moment, and he knew she was thinking suspicious thoughts. But in the end she let him help her up and they went out together.

Back inside, he put his things in the office and sat on the daybed and thought how getting her to agree that he'd stay in the house had gone pretty well. He had two weeks to get himself a better sense of Crystal as a potential wife.

He'd also get a chance to break down her defenses against the possibility that they might get married. They'd even have a kid to take care of, to practice being parents. Maybe they'd get lucky and DeDe would go back to being her old easygoing self, now that her mom and dad weren't there to fight with. Hey, it could happen.

And no matter how it all shook out in the end, at least he'd talked Crystal into this much: They were sharing a house. He only hoped the next phase of his plan would go as well as the first.

A tap on the door. "It's open."

Crystal pushed it wide. "I'm heading over to Raley's, to get some things I need for dinner."

"Great. I'll go with you."

She blinked. He was sure she would try and blow him off. But then she said, "Well, sure. If you want to."

"I'll drive."

* * *

He was up to something. Crystal knew it. Something beyond the whole weird "practice marriage" deal he'd dreamed up. She could tell by the hooded look in those eyes of his when he jumped at the chance to drive her to the grocery store.

"Raley's is that way." She pointed to the left as he turned right.

"I know where Raley's is." He made the turn and drove on in the wrong direction.

"So how come we're not going there?"

He turned his head her way and the sun glinted on the black lenses of his wraparound sunglasses. "I have something to show you first."

"What?"

He turned to face the road again. "My office."

"Why?"

"Just wait. You'll see."

She considered arguing with him, pointing out to him that she was willing to be flexible, no matter what he thought. No, she didn't want to get married just because they were having a baby. And truthfully, she didn't think the two of them would ever make a forever kind of match.

But okay, she could accept that it wouldn't hurt for the two of them to see how they got along, day-to-day, sharing the same house. Especially since the perfect opportunity to do that had fallen right in their laps.

However, his saying he wanted to go shopping with her and then heading off for somewhere else without telling her what he was up to, well, that amounted to trickery and trickery was low. And wasn't it just like him to do what he wanted and not bother to consult her?

Still. It wasn't as if she needed to be anywhere in particular at the moment. She could afford a detour, even if he *had* manipulated her into it.

Plus, she knew damned well that if she called him on his little deception, he would only start in on her about being rigid and not going with the flow. She just didn't want to hear it. So she rolled down the window, enjoyed the feel of the warm wind on her cheeks and didn't say a word the whole rest of the way to Rancho Cordova, where Tanner had his office.

The ride took about a half hour. At last, he turned into the back parking lot of a flat-roofed, unremarkable two-story building. He pulled into a space, stopped the car and took off his sunglasses.

"Ready?" There was excitement in his voice.

She almost smiled. Really, it was kind of touching how eager he seemed. "Lead the way," she said.

They went in through a rear entrance and up a flight of stairs. On the second floor, they walked down two hallways lined with doors that led to the offices of lawyers and bail bondsmen and a few businesses whose names told her nothing about what went on inside.

At last, he stopped in front of a door with Dark Horse Investigations on it and his name beneath. He unlocked that door, pushed it wide and gestured her in ahead of him.

She stepped into a reception area, which included a desk with nothing on it but a phone and a water-cooler minus the water. The lone window to the left of the desk had cheap brown miniblinds and a view of the building next door. There was brown all-weather carpeting on the floor. A brown loveseat, two end tables and a couple of brown chairs waited next to the door.

Beyond the empty desk was another door. That one had only his name on it. "I take it your private office is through there?"

He dropped to the sofa. "You got it. Want to have a look?"

"This is your deal. Do you *want* me to have a look?"

"Go for it."

So she crossed the room and opened the door on more brown carpeting, another desk—this one with a computer on top as well as a phone. Two lonely brown guest chairs faced the desk. There were four tall file cabinets filling one wall and another window with cheap blinds—that one looking out on the street in front. Framed documents marched in a line across the back wall. She moved into the room to get a closer look. The documents declared him licensed to be a private investigator in the states of California, Nevada, Oregon, Washington, Arizona and Texas.

Crystal returned to the bare waiting room, shut the door and turned to find Tanner watching her. "Depressing," she said.

"What? You don't like brown?"

"I'm surprised you ever get any clients, with an office like this."

"When you hire a P.I., it's not for the decor. And the truth is, I hardly use this place. I have a twenty-four-hour answering service. I usually just pick up my calls and meet clients…anywhere. Starbucks. Their offices. Whatever."

The phone on the desk started ringing. Tanner didn't get up.

She asked, "You're not going to answer it?"

He waited for the phone to fall silent before he explained. "The service will get it and send me a text." Right on cue, the phone at his belt chimed out two notes.

She waited for him to check the display and slide the cell back into the carrying case before she asked, "Call me crazy, but I have to know. Why have an office if you don't need it?"

He lifted a hard shoulder in a half-shrug. "Seems more…professional, I guess. An office. And an assistant. Someone to take the calls during business hours, someone to be here, to greet clients, someone to keep the records up-to-date, do the books. All that." He slanted her a look. "I have *had* assistants. They never worked out. I'm used to going it alone and they always had too many damn questions about every little thing. But I'm willing to try one more time, especially if I can find someone who likes to make her own decisions, someone who's independent by nature…."

By then it was all so painfully clear. "You mean someone like me?"

"That's right. Someone just like you."

"I don't believe it. You're offering me a job."

"Believe it. I am."

"You are just full of big plans today, aren't you?"

He gave her his broodiest look. "A man finds out he's going to be a father, it's his nature to start making plans."

She leaned back against the shut door to his brown inner sanctum. "Tell me you're kidding. You don't really imagine that you and I could work together."

"Seriously. Not kidding. I *can* imagine it. And you do need a job."

"I can't work for you."

"Why not?"

"Well, because we're having a baby."

"That's no reason. If you think about it, it's more of a reason why we *should* work together."

"No."

"Yes."

"Tanner. What matters is that we get along with each other, for the sake of the baby."

"And we are getting along, aren't we?"

"I'm saying we don't need any extra stress between us, not now."

"You mean like working together? That's going to be an extra stress?"

"It could be."

"But you don't know for certain. You won't know unless you give it a try. And you need a job. I'll be a good boss. Fair. Reasonable. And not into micromanaging."

She stared at him and wondered if there had ever been a man as exasperating as he was. At the same time, she felt such…affection toward him right then. He was trying so hard and she couldn't help but be touched by that. Still. Working for him was probably not a good idea. What if it all went to hell? They'd still have a lifelong relationship because of the baby, and they'd have to find a way to get along even if they couldn't stand each other.

She tried again to get him to see reason. "Tanner, come on. You don't need an assistant."

"Sure I do."

"If you needed one, you'd have one."

"If you say yes, I *will* have one. Come on. What can I do to convince you to give working for me a chance?"

She was running out of arguments. "Please." She went over and yanked out the swivel chair at the empty desk. It was dusty, that chair. She gave the dust a few quick swipes. "Working for you *and* living with you?" She dropped into the chair. "We'll drive each other crazy."

"You're only living with me for two weeks," he said, sounding downright cheerful. "And it's not really living together anyway, since you won't even sleep with me."

"It *is* living together, since we *are* in the same house."

He waved a hand. "Fine. We're living together. And who says we'll drive each other nuts?"

"*I* say. We've both agreed that we're not cut out to be together."

He shook his head. "Uh-uh. We covered that one back at the house. What we agreed to in the past no longer applies. And think about it this way—maybe we were wrong all along. Maybe we're both just scared to take a chance. Maybe, for the sake of the baby that's coming, we need to be braver."

Who knew the man could be so persistent? He was giving her a headache. She put her head in her hands. "Stop. Please."

He did nothing of the kind. "Who knows? This could end up being the job of a lifetime for you."

She groaned. "The job of a lifetime…" She straightened in the chair and took a long look around the ugly brown room. "You think maybe you're overplaying your hand a little here?"

In one fluid movement, he rose to his feet. "Yeah,

well. Maybe." He approached her. A too-familiar shiver went through her. She always felt like that—brimming with excitement and anticipation when he came near. He stopped beside her chair and looked down at her. His expression seemed…hopeful. So strange, Tanner Bravo looking hopeful. "You could give it a try. The hours could be flexible, for now, while you're taking care of DeDe. You could come in when she's at school. Say, six hundred a week to start. Then, if you like the job and decide to stick with it after Kelly and Mitch get back, you can go to a full forty hours at seven hundred a week."

It was more than she'd made working for the horny attorney. A lot more.

He said, "It's a job you would make up as you went along. On your own. Like I said, I don't need someone who requires a lot of hand-holding."

Impossible, but everything he'd just said appealed to her. He must have known it would: to create something from nothing, to have no rules in place that she'd feel driven to break, no antiquated systems that she had to follow because everybody in the office had always done it that way…

But no. Really. "Tanner. You're doing perfectly well the way things are now."

"I'm in a rut."

"A rut you like just fine."

"How do you know I like it?"

"Well, I just thought…"

"It's okay, the way things are now. But it could be better. Take the job. Help me out."

"But. Seven hundred a week. You have that kind of money?"

He gave her one of those looks. Patient. Weary. "You'd be surprised how much money I have. Hard work and low overhead have their advantages."

"And that's what I meant. Why add the overhead? Why not just let your lease expire here and save yourself the rent?"

He hitched a leg up on the edge of the desk and folded his hands between his knees. "You know how long I've kept this office?"

"I hate it when people answer a question with another question."

"Be patient. I *am* answering. I've had this office for five years. I kept thinking I should give it up. But I never did. Now I know why."

She shook her head. "Since I told you about the baby, you're all positive attitude and big ideas. It's pretty scary, I've gotta say."

He grinned. "Own up. You love it."

She admitted, "Well, it is kind of appealing. But how long will it last?"

He leaned toward her, dark eyes like velvet. "Forever. You watch. A lifetime, at least."

"Okay. Now I'm *really* scared." He leaned even closer. She knew then he was going to kiss her. And she wanted him to. So much. Too much. Her heart fluttered with anticipation and her cheeks felt too warm.

His lips touched hers, a brushing breath of a kiss, and the scent of him tempted her. "Say yes. Take the job." He took her by the shoulders and he rose to his feet, bringing her upright with him, pulling her closer. She let him do all that. She didn't even try to pull away.

Because she didn't *want* to pull away.

And then he kissed her again. Slower. Longer. Deeper.

She pressed herself against him. It felt so good. She kissed him back, with heat, with hunger, with real enthusiasm.

And when he finally lifted his head, she gazed dreamily up at him. "Um. What were we talking about?"

"You just agreed to work for me."

She laughed, then, and pushed him away. "You are impossible."

"But in a good way. Say yes."

She almost did. Unbelievable. Tanner had come *that* close to convincing her. Somehow, she made herself insist, "I want some time to think it over."

His eyes gleamed with triumph. "Why not? Take all the time you need."

After the trip to Raley's, Tanner helped Crystal put away the groceries, then he left to "catch up on a couple of contracts," he said. "Back by six…"

And he was gone.

The thermometer outside the kitchen window read eighty-six degrees. Crystal put on her swimsuit, grabbed a novel and went out back for a dip in the pool. She swam a few laps, then stretched out in the dappled shade of a maple with Cisco for company.

She must have drifted off to sleep because the sound of the glass slider to the family room gliding open had her stirring and lifting her head to see who was there.

It was DeDe. Cisco whined in greeting and went to her, wagging his shaggy brown tail.

Crystal hauled herself to a sitting position. "Good lesson?"

DeDe pushed the door open farther, enough that the dog could get in. "It was okay," she said glumly.

Crystal kept her bright smile in place and her tone upbeat. "Put on your suit and have a swim, why don't you?"

DeDe, who used to be the most cheerful kid on the planet, didn't so much as crack a smile. "No. I'm going to my room." She shoved the door shut without another word.

Crystal tried to decide if she ought to go after her. Giving the kid some breathing room was one thing. But if DeDe didn't snap out of it by dinner time, Crystal would have to talk to her. Maybe she could get through where Mitch and Kelly hadn't been able to.

Then again, maybe she ought to just let it go, allow DeDe the chance to deal with the problem in her own way—at least until her parents returned.

Ack. Who knew? Crystal put her hand on her stomach and silently willed her unborn baby never to be crabby or sulky or throw tantrums.

Five minutes later, the glass door opened again. Child and dog emerged. DeDe had changed to her swimsuit, after all. Her flip-flops, decorated with purple daisies, flapped against the concrete as she approached.

She dropped to the end of Crystal's chaise longue with a heavy sigh. The dog bumped her hand and she absently petted him, her expression as droopy and sad as the slump to her small shoulders.

Crystal tried a little small talk. "Did you have fun with Mia?"

"It was good," the child answered flatly. "Devon Marie and Lindsay and Alicia and Sarah Lynn came, too. We had peanut butter sandwiches. We watched *Hannah Montana* on TiVo. And we played Barbies."

"Sounds like a great time to me—and I'm glad you changed your mind about a swim. It's nice out here."

The child made a small, noncommittal sound. Then she stuck out her chin. "I like my backyard. All my friends like it, too. We had two swimming parties out here last year."

"I bet they were fun."

"They were the best. Everybody said so. And I like my house, too. Do you like my house, Crystal?" DeDe turned wide-set hazel eyes her way.

Crystal tamped down the feeling that she was about to get broadsided and gave the little girl a fond smile. "It's a great house. I love it."

"Good. You can buy it from Mom and come live here with me."

Slowly, Crystal shook her head. "Not happening. I think you know that."

"I hate the new house."

"Oh, sweetie…"

"I do. I hate it."

The Valentine family's new house, ten thousand square feet of total luxury in an exclusive gated community in nearby Elk Grove, was under construction. There would be a pool, a spa, a tennis court, a private studio where DeDe could practice her dancing, a media room, a kitchen to die for, a master suite that took up an entire wing. And lots more.

While Mitch was willing to move to the Sacramento area and start up something new there on the business front, he insisted that his family have the kind of enormous, showy, state-of-the-art house he could easily afford. Kelly was fine with the move and excited about working to make it the home of her dreams. She loved meeting with the architect and the builder. She'd had a ball interviewing potential interior designers and kept promising Mitch she'd choose one soon.

DeDe, on the other hand, was miserable. "Why do we have to move?" she whined. "I don't want to move." And the tears started in again, welling up, spilling down her round cheeks.

"DeDe. Listen. It's not going to do any good to—"

A wail cut her off. "I live *here*," DeDe sobbed, flinging her arms up and then bringing them down hard. The chaise shook. "I've always lived here. But now that my dad's come back, I have to move away and leave all my friends and go to a new school—some fancy private school that's supposed to be so much better than my old school, which is a *good* school. Everyone says so. But no. Now *he's* here and everything has to be all different. Sometimes I hate him…."

"Oh, DeDe. No…"

"I do. I hate him!" DeDe jumped to her feet on a sob. "Sometimes I wish he'd just stayed away. I know that's wrong and bad. But I don't care. My dad came back and it ruined my life!"

Chapter Five

Tanner called at five to six. "This is going to take a little longer than I thought. I'll miss dinner."

"Gee, and I was going to burn it especially for you."

His low laughter warmed her. "Now I really feel bad."

"Thanks for calling."

"No problem. Everything okay there?"

"DeDe burst into tears and said she hates Mitch. Then she ran to her room. She's been in there ever since."

He swore low. "You want me there? I can—"

"No. I'm fine, really. She stormed off to her room at a little after four. It's been nice and peaceful around here since then."

"You sure you're all right on your own?"

"Positive."

"Back by eight."

"That's fine." She hung up feeling all domestic and warm-fuzzy. He really did seem to be taking this experiment in living together seriously, making the time to call and let her know when he was going to be late, even volunteering to cut work short if she couldn't handle DeDe on her own.

She hummed a little tune under her breath and pulled open the flatware drawer.

Then, with a frown, she shoved it shut. Setting the table was Deirdre's job. Yes, it was tempting to just let the kid stay in her room and sulk to her heart's content, to consider it a long time-out.

But dinner was important. And so was making sure a child did all her regular chores. Tantrums shouldn't be rewarded by the chance to shirk household responsibilities.

Crystal turned and marched through the dining room, into the hall to the shut door of DeDe's room, which was decorated with painted-on daisies and pictures of her favorite Disney Channel stars. There was also a flag with the name of her school on it and a big black rectangular sticker with Private on it, a skull and crossbones beneath. Daisies grew out of the eyes of that skull, a little touch of nine-year-old whimsy that made Crystal smile in spite of how much she didn't want to deal with an acting-out preteen right at that moment.

She lifted her hand and gave the door a rap.

Total silence within. She knocked again.

And at last there was a sour-sounding, "What?"

Crystal pushed the door open. Inside, the walls were purple and hung with posters of pop stars and world-famous ballerinas. DeDe, who'd changed to a short blue dress and leggings, sat cross-legged on the bed reading a magazine, iPod earbuds stuck in her ears. She glared at Crystal and asked, "What?"—again.

Crystal waited until, with a snort of annoyance, she took off the earbuds.

"What?" she demanded for the third time.

"Do you have any clue how rude you're being?"

DeDe tried for defiance—and ended up just looking miserable. "I'm sorry, okay? I know it's not your fault."

Crystal left the doorway and entered the room. Pushing a pile of magazines aside, she sat on the bed next to DeDe. "What you said about hating your dad…"

DeDe hung her head. "I know. That was bad. And I didn't mean it. I don't hate him. I love him."

"I know you do."

"But I'm just…so mad at him! He's the one that went away. And now he's back and everything has to change to be like *he* wants it…."

Crystal dealt with the main truth. "You know he never would have gone away if he'd known about you. It was…a special situation. He left town. And then he changed his name because he wanted to change his life. And your mom couldn't find him to tell him about you."

"Yeah. I know all that. He and Mom told me the whole story. But still. When he came back, I told him I didn't want to go and live other places. He said he would stay here."

"And he did. He's moved here. He has homes in Texas and Los Angeles, but now he lives here, in Sacramento."

"No. That's not what I meant. I meant here, at my *house*. I don't want to move away from my house or my friends or my school. And he knows it, too."

Crystal had no idea how far she should take this discussion. It was, in the end, a problem for DeDe and her mom and dad to solve. "Listen." She reached out, brushed a hand down DeDe's shining, straight hair. DeDe allowed that, which Crystal found encouraging. "You're here now, at your house, just the way you want to be, right?"

DeDe wrinkled up her nose. "Uh. Duh." She shook her head. "Crystal, you are cool and you look like a magic princess."

"Why, thank you."

"But sometimes you say weird things."

Crystal stifled a laugh. "What's weird about saying that you're here now."

"Uh. Because I know that already and so it's not something I need to have you tell me."

"But maybe it is. Maybe you're forgetting that you're here, now."

"Oh. Come. On." DeDe drooped her shoulders and rolled her eyes. "Like that I live here is something I could forget."

Crystal did laugh, then. "Listen. Focus."

"Fine. Whatever."

"Have you thought about how, while you're being so mad all the time about what's going to happen months from now, you're not enjoying what *is* happening now?"

"But how can I enjoy it? I can't stop thinking that I'm going to have to move away!"

"Yes, you are going to be moving. But right now, today, you're living in your house just the way you want to be. You're going to the school you've always gone to, and you're hanging with your forever friends, going to all your regular dance classes, playing Barbies and watching the Disney Channel on TiVo."

DeDe *was* listening now. Her wide brow had furrowed and she sat with her elbows on her spread knees, her chin canted forward. "Yeah. So?"

"So, right now you've got everything you want. And later, when you move, this wonderful time in your life will be over, never to come again. Are you going to look back on it and remember that you were mad and sulking most of the time—or are you going to remember what a great time you had, that you didn't waste a minute throwing tantrums and being angry at everyone?"

The question hung in the air. Finally, DeDe said, "Well, I…"

"You what?"

"Okay," DeDe said grudgingly. "I'll try not to be so mad all the time."

Crystal resisted the urge to give her the famous Yoda quote: "Do or do not. There is no 'try.'" She figured the nine-year-old had endured enough philosophizing for one evening. "Good, then. Wash your hands and set the table."

DeDe was subdued through the meal but not hostile. Afterward, without being reminded, she cleared off the dishes and loaded the dishwasher. She asked Crystal to play *Super Mario Galaxy* on Wii with her, and Crystal happily agreed. Within ten minutes, they were both laughing and having a great time.

Tanner appeared at a little before eight.

DeDe turned to him eagerly. "Uncle Tanner! Come and play with us."

He gave her one of his slow smiles. "In a minute."

He sent Crystal a look that made her wish they were sharing a bedroom, after all. "Any dinner left?"

"In the fridge. It's probably cold by now…."

"No problem. I'll give it a zap."

He ate and then came and played with them. Crystal got the warm-fuzzies again. She tried not to look at him with stars in her eyes, imagining what it might be like if they did work it out and somehow managed to make a family together….

For once in her life, she knew she had to keep both feet on the ground. For over two months she and Tanner had been constantly agreeing that they were *not* meant for each other. And now, in the space of a day, they were staying in the same house and she was considering going to work for him. It was too much, too soon, even for a woman who liked to take life as it came.

At nine-thirty, with DeDe in bed, Crystal made a beeline for the guest room. She shut the door, leaned against it and hoped that Tanner wouldn't come knocking, insisting that they spend the evening together.

Uh-uh. They'd been together for more than half the day. It was enough for now. It was too much.

He was too tempting, too sexy, too determined, too…everything. She needed a break from him, or who knew what might happen? She could end up agreeing to whatever he wanted—or at the very least, having sex with him. And sex right now seemed somehow inappropriate. Partly because of having DeDe in the house. And partly because Crystal pretty much lost her mind when she had sex with Tanner. She became a slave to her own pleasure.

And how undignified was that?

Uh-uh. Tonight was a great night to go it alone. Take some time for rest and reflection.

The guest room was just about ideal as a retreat. Mitch had used it for his room when he first came back to Sacramento, after he knew he had a daughter but before he and Kelly had reconciled. It had a top-quality mattress on the king-sized bed and a big flatscreen television. And its own private bathroom—without a tub. But hey. She'd make do with a long, hot shower.

Crystal took her shower and put on her big pink sleep shirt with Peace. Love. Chocolate. written on the front in lipstick-red letters.

Chocolate. Hmm. She'd bought a bag of her favorite Dove dark chocolate at the grocery store that day. Those little individual ones with the message inside the wrapper of each chocolate. She really liked those messages. Like getting your fortune told along with a delicious bite of your favorite dark, rich, oh-so-creamy treat.

Too bad she'd left the bag out in the pantry closet...

Or tea. Some nice herb tea would be perfect about now. Tea, with a little of that sage honey she'd bought that afternoon when she convinced Tanner to make a stop at the natural foods co-op.

Crystal shook her head. Firmly. Come on. She was going to be a mother, for heaven's sake. She needed to stop being led around by her appetites.

All of them. Chocolate. Tea. And sex with Tanner, too.

She climbed up on the bed and sat lotus-style and closed her eyes and tried to clear her mind of all thought. She took deep, slow, even breaths.

But in the end, her mind would not be cleared. It was full of all kinds of random, self-indulgent thoughts. Her mind was all about chocolate and steaming, fragrant tea. About sex. And about how she was hiding in her room, really. Hiding from Tanner.

And how mature was that?

Not very.

She pulled on a robe over the sleep shirt, opened the door to the hallway and stuck her head out. Silence. The door to DeDe's room was shut. To her left at the end of the hall, the door to the master suite stood open, darkness beyond. She couldn't see the door to the office Tanner was using as a bedroom. It was around the corner to her right, in the front hall. From the dining room and beyond, all was darkness. Tanner must have gone out or gone to bed.

How silly of her to have tried to avoid him. Especially when it ended up being totally unnecessary. She could get her tea and chocolate and return to her room with it. Turn on that nice flatscreen and veg out to E! or maybe find some great tearjerker on Lifetime.

She padded along the hall, through the dark dining room and into the kitchen, where she flipped on a mellow under-counter light and put the water on for tea. Humming to herself, she went into the laundry room and got the bag of chocolate from the pantry closet. She was just shutting the pantry door and turning for the kitchen when a tall, broad-shouldered figure loomed up before her in the open doorway.

She let out a semishriek. It was a ridiculously wimpy sound, like the squeal of a cornered mouse, and dropped the bag of candy, only then realizing that the tall figure was Tanner.

She blew out a hard breath of total aggravation and

bent to retrieve the chocolate. "In case you didn't know, you just scared a decade off my life."

"Sorry. But I was starting to think you were going to stay locked in your room all night." He flipped on the light to the laundry room. The small space burst into brightness.

She blinked against the sudden glare. "I considered staying in my room," she nobly replied. "But then I decided it was beneath me."

"Good."

She clutched the bag of chocolate to her chest. "So you've been sitting around in the dark, waiting for me to appear so you could ambush me?"

He dismissed her with a look. "That's over-dramatizing."

"But true."

She got a shrug for an answer.

"A cheap little deception," she said in a lofty tone.

"Yeah, and it worked just fine."

She tried glaring at him. But he only gazed steadily back at her. So she gave up the superior attitude and sighed. "So now I'm out. Happy?" She took a step forward. When he didn't move aside, she muttered darkly, "Excuse me." And he finally got out of the way. She flicked the light off again as she went by it, carried her bag of chocolate to the table and set it down. "I'm having tea. Want some?"

"No, thanks. Not a tea man. Maybe a beer." He went to the fridge and helped himself, then took a chair at the table as she got down a narrow canister of herb tea and put a teabag in a mug.

He was so quiet behind her. She could feel his eyes, watching, practically burning twin holes in her back.

When the mug was ready for the water, she turned and leaned against the counter. "I hope you're not going to start in on me about the job again. It's only been a few hours since you offered it to me. I haven't made my mind up yet."

"No. Take your time about the job." He tipped his beer at the chair beside him. "Have a seat."

"As soon as the water boils." Ridiculous, but she felt safer across the room from him. "So. What?"

He set the beer down on the table and then stared at it, suddenly somber. "I want to know more about you."

She swallowed. Her heart pounded faster than it should, which was silly. "What, exactly, do you want to know?"

"Everything."

She put her hand to her throat, a self-protective gesture—and then realized how the move betrayed her. She let it drop to her side.

He said, "You're having my baby. And I don't know enough about you. You've never said where you grew up, who your parents were, any of that...." His voice trailed off.

She tried to think what to say to him. Nothing came. And Tanner just sat there. Watching her. Waiting.

Yesterday, she'd been so certain that she'd be going it alone, a single mom. But who knew that Tanner Bravo would be so determined to make her see otherwise? He really did seem to want to create a family with her—and not just because he considered marrying her the "right" thing to do. He honestly seemed to believe it was the *best* thing to do, that they could make a go of it, the two of them and the baby.

And that terrified her. Almost as much as it made her feel all warm and safe inside. And hopeful, too.

The man had her head spinning with fear that it wouldn't work out between them. And with the glowing, impossible hope that it might.

Into the extended silence, he repeated, "Growing up, Crys. You never talk about it."

And right then, at that exact moment, something shifted within her. She saw that she really did have a responsibility to him. If there was to be any chance for the two of them—and she was discovering that she did want that chance—she was going to need to tell him the stuff she hated to talk about.

She met his eyes directly. "You're right. I don't talk about growing up. It wasn't a great time in my life."

He sipped from his beer, set the bottle down. "I know what you mean. As a kid, my life wasn't so great, either."

Kelly had told her a little about how rough they'd had it as children. "So…maybe *you* should tell *me* about that, huh?"

"I will," he said, "if you want to hear it."

"I do want to hear it—in fact, now would be good."

He wasn't going for it. "Come on." His voice had gentled. "You're doing great. Don't chicken out on me."

More possible evasions scrolled through her brain. She didn't fall prey to them. She answered him honestly, letting the old wounds show. "Maybe I'm only lying to myself, but…I like to think I've remade myself, you know? That I'm not the same person anymore. I've made a new life. I've changed my name."

He frowned. "Just like Mitch, huh?"

"Yeah. It's how we became friends, in a way. We understood each other, Mitch and me. We both walked away from impossible situations, and we both re-created ourselves."

"So Mitch knows all this stuff you haven't told me?"

Was that jealousy she saw in his eyes? Lately, he and Mitch seemed to have worked out their differences. But there had been some serious animosity between them in the past. Mitch had felt that Tanner "stole" Kelly from him a decade ago, when she chose to move to Fresno with her newly found brother and left Mitch behind. Tanner had considered Mitch a total loser for making Kelly choose between the two of them.

She explained, "Mitch doesn't know the details. Only that I left my past behind and changed my name, the same as he did."

"So, your name isn't Crystal?"

"Yes, it is." She knew she sounded defensive. Angry—which she was. "Don't ever say it's not."

He frowned. "Whoa. That's a sore spot, huh?"

The fight drained out of her. She spoke levelly. "Crystal Cerise is my legal name and has been since I was eighteen. It's just not the name I was born with."

"What was your name, before?"

"God. You *had* to ask."

"Come on. It can't be that bad...." His tone was tender. Coaxing.

"It's just that I hate my given name, that's all. I've always hated it."

"Tell me." He said it gently, but still it was a command.

She gritted her teeth and made herself do it. "Martha. Martha Cunningham." The name—once her own—felt so strange, alien, on her lips now.

"Martha," he repeated softly.

She glared at him. "I'll warn you now. Never call me that. I know there are many lovely women named Martha. No offense to them, but to me, Martha Cunningham sounds like the name of the mother in a fifties sitcom. Plus, when I was Martha, my life was a mess. So swear you won't call me that—not even when you're teasing me."

He put up a hand. "Crystal, I swear."

She pressed her lips together, nodded. "Thank you."

"No problem. Go on—your childhood. Your parents. I want to know about all that."

It did seem important now, a major step, to give him the bare facts, at least. "I was an only kid and my parents, especially my dad, were very strict. There was…no laughter, you know? No fun. No color in our house. My parents were Christians but the kind of Christians who give a beautiful, forgiving religion—a religion of hope and redemption—a very bad name. They were cold. And judgmental. And they were beyond frugal. My dad knew how to stretch every penny until it screamed for mercy. My mom bought all my clothes in secondhand stores, even though they could have afforded new things." She gave a low laugh. "I'm sure that's why I've made it almost a point of pride to live in the moment, never to worry about where the next paycheck is coming from."

"You were always at odds with your mom and dad, then?"

"Not always. When I was little, I tried so hard to please them. But somehow, nothing I did was good enough. As time went on, I started to rebel. I got into trouble. With drugs. With the wrong group of kids. With…" She chickened out, let the word trail off into silence. She just wasn't ready to get into the hardest part.

He asked what she knew he would ask. "With what?"

She glanced toward the dark doorway to the laundry room and said nothing. He took the hint and didn't ask again.

In time, she continued. "I left home when I was seventeen. Ran away, after a huge fight with my father. He said he was through with me. He and my mom'd had enough of trying to deal with me. So I left. And never came back."

"Where did all this happen?" he asked.

"You mean, where did I grow up?" She waited for his nod before confessing, "Here, in Northern California. In Roseville, to be specific."

He frowned. "Less than thirty miles away from here."

"Right."

"So when you decided to move to Sacramento…"

She nodded. "It wasn't only because I thought Mitch might need me, though that honestly was a big part of it. It's been eight years since I walked away from my mother and father and swore I would never look back. But lately, in the past year or so…"

"You want to work things out with them?"

She made a low, pained sound and shook her head. "No way. Unless they've changed a whole lot, there's not going to be any working things out. But I do find myself wondering, if maybe they *have* changed. I want…I don't know. I only…"

The whistle of the kettle cut her off. And she was grateful for it, for the excuse to turn away from those knowing eyes of his, to go about the simple task of pouring the steaming water into her mug, of carrying the mug and spoon to the table, of getting out the honey to sweeten the hot brew.

She felt his gaze on her, quiet and watchful, as she performed the mundane actions.

When she finally settled into the chair next to him, he prompted, "You only, what?"

She cupped a hand around the side of her mug. The heat was soothing. "I'm…working up to it, to contacting them again."

He reached out, brushed a hand along her arm. A gesture of—what?—companionship? Encouragement?

A smile kind of wobbled its way across her mouth. "So all right. How was it for you, as a kid?"

He regarded her without speaking for a count of at least ten. Then he said, "I was born right here in Sacramento. My mother was a sometime-waitress and hotel maid named Lia Wells. My dad was Blake Bravo. I suppose you've heard about him…."

Everyone knew the story of Blake Bravo. The man was a legend—and not in a good way. He had kidnapped his own nephew for a ransom in diamonds. That was after he faked his own death to avoid a manslaughter rap. He'd lived under the radar, never getting caught by the police, for almost thirty years. During that time, he had children by a number of women all over the country.

Tanner said, "My mother always claimed he married her. But so did all the women he had children with—or so most of my half-siblings say. When my mother got pregnant with me, Blake left her. He returned a few years later, got her pregnant with Kelly. And left again. My mother put us in foster care, separately, when Kelly was just a baby and I was four years old—and neglected to tell either of us that we had a sibling. Then she had

Hayley." Crystal had yet to meet Hayley. She lived with her husband and child in Seattle. Tanner said, "My mother did the same with Hayley—put her in the system, didn't tell her about me and Kelly, didn't tell Kelly or me about her. Our mother wouldn't let us go, give us up to be adopted, to belong to another family. But she wouldn't take responsibility for us, either."

A shiver went through Crystal. As Tanner talked of his mother, her own past was suddenly there, before her, complete with all the heartbreak, with the choice that had been forced on her, the choice she despised to this day.

She heard herself asking, "Do you hate her, your mother?"

"She's dead now," he said.

Crystal knew she should let it go. But somehow, she couldn't. "I know she's dead. But do you hate her?"

He took a minute to mull over the question. "No," he finally said. "She was weak. And messed up. I think I hated her at least a little when I was small and had to live with her deserting me. But I'm over that now."

Crystal asked yet another question she knew she shouldn't ask. "Would you have liked it better if she'd let you go, let you be adopted?"

"I don't know. Can't answer that. It didn't happen. If it had, and I'd ended up with a kind, loving family, I might have been a more cheerful kind of guy. But maybe I'd never have found my sisters."

Crystal didn't believe that for a second. "Oh, no. You would have found them. One way or another."

He watched her from under hooded brows. "You think so?"

"I know so. I know that much about you. And go on. Please."

His chuckle was low and without much humor. "You're kidding. Haven't you heard enough?"

"Uh-uh. Go on."

And he did. "So I grew up in foster care. I hated it, more than I ever hated my mother. I hated the group homes and I hated the families who took me in and tried to take care of me. I had a bad attitude, and that's an understatement. My parents had pretty much thrown me away, at least my father had. My mother had, too—just without letting me go. As soon as I graduated high school, I joined the army for two years. When I got out, I moved to Fresno, went to college part-time on the GI bill and started working for a bail bondsman to put food on the table. I found out I had a sister a year later by badgering my mother without mercy when she was sick."

"Kelly told me that you always knew you had a sister, that you remembered her, remembered there had been a baby before your mom put you into the group home, even though you were only four when Kelly was born."

"Right. Too bad I had no clue about Hayley, which is why we didn't find her till last year, when Lia died." He'd been staring into the middle distance, but now he looked straight at her. "You just said Kelly's told you all this."

"She told me about how you found her, yes. And some about your mom. And Blake. But I wanted to hear it from you, to hear how you felt about it all, how it affected you."

"You did, huh?" He sounded…what? Amused, maybe. Or even pleased.

"Yes." There was one of those moments. They gazed

at each other in a quiet that seemed to shimmer with expectation, with excitement. And heat. Was it possible that they had gotten past a boundary, somehow, broken through to another level, just by telling each other a little about how they started out, how they got to where they were now?

Crystal knew it was only talk. But it was *important* talk, stuff that people who were in an actual relationship needed to tell each other.

He reached out and caught her hand. As always, she responded instantly to his touch. A warm shiver of awareness traveled up her arm and then straight down into her belly, where it bloomed into heat.

"Come here." He spoke in a rough whisper.

The thing was, she wanted to go there. She wanted to go wherever he wanted to take her. It somehow always came down to that, between the two of them.

She shook her head. "We shouldn't." But she failed to pull her hand away.

He gave a tug. And not a very hard one. She rose and turned and ended up exactly where he wanted her—in his lap. He nuzzled her neck. It felt really good.

"I can't believe I'm sitting on your lap."

"Believe it." He went on kissing her neck.

"If DeDe wakes up—"

"She won't. And you smell good." He groaned, low. It was a happy, sexy kind of sound. Beneath her hips, he was hardening.

She wiggled a little, just to torment him. He groaned again, and bit the side of her neck—lightly. "Ouch," she said, and sighed with pleasure.

He licked the spot his teeth had grazed. "You taste good, too...."

"You always say that."

"Because it's true."

She shifted around, causing him to groan some more, until she could capture his mouth. They shared a kiss. A long and lovely one.

But then, every kiss she'd ever shared with him was a lovely one, each in its own way. She cuddled in close to him, tucking her head against his shoulder.

"I can't believe the things I told you tonight," she whispered. "I don't talk about that time of my life. Ever."

"But now you have." He sounded proud.

Her robe had fallen open, parting wide across her legs. He stroked her bare thigh, his fingers wandering higher as he captured her mouth again. She wore no panties—not to bed. And she *had* been in bed before she crept out here in the dark seeking tea and chocolate.

And getting so much more than she'd bargained for.

He touched her, his palm gliding like rough silk on the flesh of her inner thigh, his thumb brushing the curls that covered her sex. It felt so good. She made a low, pleasured sound and eased her thighs wider apart, giving him better access. His thumb moved again, parting her, sliding along the secret place that was already slick and wet for him. He made a growling sound of male arousal.

Somewhere in the back of her mind, a voice nagged that she was not supposed to be doing this, that she'd told him they weren't sleeping together while they were here at Kelly's, and what kind of a marshmallow did that make her if she ended up sharing a bed with him the very first night they stayed there?

And more important than anything else, what about DeDe?

As if on cue, as she thought the child's name, she heard the soft creak of a door opening somewhere on the other side of the house. Tanner must have heard it, too. They pulled back in unison.

He whispered, "Did you hear—"

She didn't wait for him to finish the question, but leaped off his lap and back to her own chair. Tanner scooted his legs under the table to hide the obvious bulge in the front of his pants.

They heard the sound of bare feet approaching. Crystal was smoothing her robe together over her thighs when DeDe appeared in the doorway to the dining room.

"What are you guys doing in here?" She squinted at them suspiciously. Her hair was tangled into a knot on one side of her head and she had a sleep mark on her cheek. She wore purple pedal-length pajamas.

Tanner held up his nearly empty bottle of Bud. "Havin' a beer."

Crystal raised her mug. "And tea…"

DeDe squinted all the harder. She looked from Tanner to Crystal and back at her uncle again. "In the dark?"

Crystal considered arguing that it wasn't dark, that the under-counter lights provided a nice, soft glow. But she knew that would only sound defensive and guilty. Which she was. Defensive. And guilty as original sin.

Tanner didn't fool around making excuses. "Go back to bed. It's late."

DeDe planted her feet in a wider stance, folded her arms across her flat chest and demanded, "Tell the truth. You guys are dating, aren't you?"

Chapter Six

Bust-ed.

Crystal could have kicked herself. She'd been sitting on his *lap,* for heaven's sake. And what about those kisses?—the deep, wet, lingering kind. And that thumb of his. There was no excuse for what his thumb had been doing.

With a troubled, curious nine-year-old sleeping down the hall, what his thumb had been doing was the pinnacle of inappropriateness.

Just their luck that Tanner's niece was way too perceptive for a nine-year-old. *Are you guys dating?* What in the world were they supposed to say to that?

Tanner saved her the trouble of coming up with a response. He went literal. "No. We're not dating." And Crystal hid her smile of relief as she realized that technically he was telling the truth. They were lovers. They were going to be parents together. But they'd yet to go out on a single date.

All of which was going to be a little tough to explain to DeDe when Crystal got so far along that there would be no hiding her pregnancy from curious nine-year-old eyes. But since it was the kind of thing a mother would deal with, the job would fall to Kelly. Crystal was beyond grateful for that.

"Not dating…" DeDe didn't look convinced. "You sure?"

"Absolutely," Tanner answered dryly. "Now, go back to bed."

DeDe flipped a hank of tangled hair back over her shoulder. "Well, I was just wondering, you know? I mean, nobody tells me *anything* around here. I'm just the kid who has to do what the grown-ups want even if it's wrong and not fair and not what my dad promised."

"Bed," said Tanner. "Now."

"Well, what if I have to go the bathroom or something?"

Tanner only looked at her.

She blew out a breath. "Fine. All right. Going." And she stomped off the way she'd come. They heard a door shut sharply. And then they both waited for the sounds that told them she was finished in the bathroom.

A few minutes later, they heard her go to her own room and shut that door. Loudly.

Tanner finished off his beer. "See how she did that? Shut that door just hard enough that she wasn't quite slamming it?" He shook his head.

"This calls for chocolate." She reached for her bag of candy and tried to pull it open. When it wouldn't give, he took it from her and did the job effortlessly.

He handed it back. "I thought you didn't eat things with sugar in them."

"Balance," she said serenely. "Balance is all. Everything in moderation."

"Woo-woo to you, too." He saluted her with his empty beer.

She took a chocolate and removed the red foil wrapper. The message inside said: *Naughty can be nice.* Yeah, right. She popped the treat into her mouth and sucked on it gratefully. The lovely creamy texture soothed her. "Yum. I could eat a mountain of these."

"But you won't, right?" he muttered. "That wouldn't be balanced."

"Exactly. And we shouldn't have been kissing, not right here in the kitchen where she can walk in on us at any time. We shouldn't have been kissing and we shouldn't have been…" She waved a hand. "You know."

"Oh, yeah. I know." He seemed very pleased with himself. "So what do you say? My room—or your room, where the bed is bigger?"

"Not going to happen. And you should wipe that smirk off your face. It's really not funny. Not funny at all."

"I'm not smirking. I swear it."

"She might have caught us in the act, so to speak. Then what would we have said? I'm serious. We really have to watch ourselves."

"You're right," he said solemnly.

She didn't lecture him further. He seemed to have gotten the message. At least for the moment.

* * *

The next day, Sunday, Tanner slept late. Crystal and DeDe had breakfast together. Once the meal was cleared off, Crystal checked the calendar on the fridge.

She turned to DeDe. "Homework time."

DeDe shrugged. "No problem. I'll do it tonight."

Crystal considered letting it go. But no. The instructions were clear. "Go on. Get it over with."

DeDe made a long-suffering noise in her throat. "But I always finish my homework at night, after dinner...."

Crystal pointed to the calendar. "What does it say there?"

DeDe glanced to the side, to the ceiling, at the floor—anywhere but where Crystal was pointing. "What do you *mean?*"

Crystal rapped her knuckles on the fridge door. "Read it," she commanded.

DeDe assumed an expression of great patience. "Well, you don't have to get mad at me."

"Read it."

"Oh, fine. *Homework after breakfast.* So?"

"So, correct me if I'm wrong, but I believe that was breakfast we just had. And this would be *after.* So go get it done."

DeDe put on her most wounded expression. "You don't have to treat me like I'm stupid."

Crystal said, too quietly, "You are to do your homework after breakfast today. And that means now."

"But that calendar is only to *remind* me, you know? As long as I get it done, I don't see what it matters when, exactly, I do it."

At that moment, Crystal wished Tanner would hurry up and get out of bed. She seriously needed backup and Tanner was pretty good at getting through to his niece—and there was a thought. How would he handle this? She knew instantly: one-word sentences.

"Homework." She tried to imitate Tanner's flat delivery. "Now."

"But I—"

"DeDe. Now."

Kelly's daughter slumped her shoulders, stuck out her chin and let out a long groan of misery. But she did turn around and head for her room.

Crystal sank into a chair and wished she was anywhere but there, being endlessly tortured by DeDe Valentine, who used to be such a nice little girl.

Tanner, in sweats and an old T-shirt, appeared in the doorway to the living room. He yawned and stretched and then leaned against the doorframe, crossing those beautiful, muscular arms over his lean chest. "Did someone let an elephant loose in the house?"

Crystal sent him a look of infinite weariness. "No, that was just DeDe, stomping off down the hall to do her homework under protest."

He yawned again. "And she used to be such a nice kid, too."

"My thoughts, exactly."

He went to her and tipped her chin up with a finger. She looked up his strong torso into those dark-chocolate eyes and wanted to lift the hem of that ratty T-shirt a little and press her lips to his washboard belly. But if she did, DeDe would probably appear out of nowhere and demand they admit they were going out together. She caught his hand, gave it an affectionate squeeze and gently pushed him away.

He didn't seem offended at her backing him off. "I'm free today," he said. "You?"

She laughed. "Well, as free as I can be, considering I'm trapped in the same house with a preteen mysteriously possessed by demons."

He went to the counter, got coffee beans from a cabinet and spooned them into the grinder. "We can hang out by the pool. Or maybe go over to Land Park, throw a Frisbee around, give Cisco some exercise." The dog, stretched out in the corner, perked up his good ear at the mention of his name. Then Tanner turned on the grinder. The loud noise filled the kitchen.

When the grinding stopped, Crystal realized that the phone was ringing. She got up and grabbed the cordless extension from its cradle on the china hutch.

DeDe had already picked it up. Crystal heard her mutter, "Hello?" How did the kid manage to sound hostile just saying hello?

"Hi, honey." It was Kelly.

Quietly, Crystal hung up. Maybe it would help DeDe's attitude a little to have a few minutes alone on the phone with her mom.

Tanner quirked a brow at her. "Kelly," she said. "DeDe answered it."

He poured the grounds into the basket, put the water in the reservoir and pushed the button to brew. "Want some eggs?"

Eggs made her nauseous lately, though she'd always

liked them well enough before she got pregnant. "I ate, thanks."

He got out bacon and the eggs and bread for toast. The scent of brewing coffee filled the kitchen as he laid strips of bacon on Kelly's electric griddle.

Crystal was just thinking how pleasant it was, relaxing on a Sunday morning, sipping her tea, watching the hunk who happened to be the father of her baby as he made his breakfast.

"Crystal!" She winced as DeDe bellowed from down the hall. "Phone! It's Mom!"

Crystal picked up the cordless extension again. "Hello?" She heard the click as DeDe got off the line.

"Hey," said Kelly. "How're you holding up?"

"Just fine," she replied firmly.

"DeDe's not giving you fits yet?"

"Nope. Doing great." Her gaze strayed to Tanner again. He gave her a wink. "Your brother's staying here, after all. Helping out."

"Good." Kelly's tone held no questions. She remained totally oblivious to what was going on between her best friend and her big brother. "I know my daughter's a handful these days, but she loves her Uncle Tanner. I have a feeling you'll be glad he's there."

"He's...very much appreciated." She sent him a grin and he saluted her with the spatula he was using to separate the bacon. "So are you tan and rested yet?"

Kelly laughed. "Give me a minute, will you? We just got here." She launched into a description of their luxury hotel suite and the white-sand beaches she could see from their balcony. It was evening there now. They were going to a party under the stars where they'd enjoy the local cuisine and dance until dawn.

"I'm green with envy," said Crystal. "Have the best time of your life."

"Oh, we intend to. Mitch says hi."

"Give him my love. Tell him to spoil you."

"He is."

"Excellent."

"Don't be afraid to ground my daughter if you have to," Kelly said sternly. "And call. Seriously. If there's anything…"

"I will, I promise. Want to say hi to Tanner?" She sent him a questioning glance. He shrugged.

"Just send our love," said Kelly.

Crystal hung up. The bacon sizzled on the grill. She didn't eat pork as a rule, but it smelled amazing. "Your sister loves you—and I think I'll have some of that bacon."

"I thought you hated pork."

"I never said I hated it. It's not my favorite, that's all. Many religions consider pork to be unclean. I respect that."

"So do I. More for me."

"You are such a philistine."

"That's me all over. And I love me some bacon."

She laughed. "Yeah, well. All at once, so do I. Please may I have some of your bacon?"

Dark eyes gleamed. "And a pickle?"

"Oh, yeah. With ice cream…"

Two hours later, DeDe was still in her room with the door closed. Crystal went to check on her and found her hooked up to her iPod, reading *Popstar!* magazine and eating Conversation Hearts.

Crystal asked to see the finished homework.

DeDe groaned. "Oh, please. I'm doing it. Soon."

"Have you even started yet?"

"I told you. Soon."

"You haven't even started it. Is that what you're telling me?"

"Crystal. I will. Soon."

Crystal held out her hand. "iPod, magazine, Conversation Hearts. Please."

"But Crys-taaall…"

"And your phone, too. Now."

With much snorting and groaning, DeDe handed over the requested items. "And *now* what'm I s'posed to do?"

"Your homework. And the good news is, you'll have plenty of time to do it because you are grounded for the rest of the day."

"What?" It was a cry of pure outrage. "You can't ground me."

"I just did."

"But…I want to go over to Lindsay's later. We're going to—"

"No. Actually, you're not doing anything with Lindsay because you are staying in your room." On that note, Crystal bowed out quickly and shut the door.

She knew with hideous certainty that DeDe would follow, yanking the door wide, storming out into the hallway, screaming and stomping her feet—at which point, Crystal would be faced with having to think up some even more dire punishment than being grounded.

But luck was with her. There was one final cry of outrage from the other side of the door—and silence.

Crystal didn't have time to enjoy the relief. Out of

nowhere, her stomach heaved. She clutched DeDe's stuff to her chest and breathed in slowly through her nose.

Didn't help.

Clamping a hand over her mouth, she whirled for her own room, where she tossed DeDe's things on the bed and raced into the bathroom. She dropped to her knees and threw back the toilet seat in the nick of time.

The heaving started. It was not pretty. When she thought it was over, she flushed. And then it happened again. She hurled some more and flushed a second time.

Finally, as she sagged over the bowl, hoping that maybe it was truly over at last, Tanner spoke from behind her.

"How you doin'?"

She groaned. "Guess."

"Not real good?"

She pointed behind her. "Shut the door to the hallway, would you? DeDe…"

"You got it." He left. She heard the door click shut in the other room. And then he returned. "What can I do?"

She started to rise. He was right there to help her. She let herself lean on him. Why not? It felt good to lean on him. "Thanks. I'll be okay, now." Two steps and she was at the sink. She rinsed out her mouth. It wasn't enough. She grabbed her toothbrush and squirted some paste on it.

He waited while she brushed her teeth. When she stuck the brush back in the holder, he reached for her.

She turned to him with a sigh and let him hold her, let herself sag against him, let herself feel cherished and protected in his big, strong arms.

He stroked her hair. "Better?"

"Ugh," she said into his T-shirt. "Two weeks of worrying myself sick about how I was going to tell you what you deserved to know. And then losing my job. And then finally *managing* to tell you. All that, and I never threw up. It took DeDe Valentine to get me down on my knees hugging the toilet bowl."

He chuckled and kissed the top of her head. "Chin up. You're doing great."

She raised her head and met his eyes. "Yeah, but Mitch and Kelly've been gone barely twenty-four hours. I may not survive another thirteen days of this."

"Any time you want me to deal with her..."

"Thanks." She leaned her head on his shoulder again. "And if you're there when she starts acting out, be my guest. Please. But you know, it's getting to be a point of honor to handle it myself when it's just her and me."

"This is the worst of it." His deep voice rumbled under her ear. "She's testing you. When she sees you won't give in to her, she'll lighten up."

"Oh, Tanner. I hope you're right."

Chapter Seven

DeDe stayed in her room the rest of the day, only emerging for meals, which she ate in stony silence.

At dinner, Tanner asked her if she'd done her homework yet.

"I did it *hours* ago." DeDe turned to Crystal. "So can I have my phone back now, and my iPod?"

Crystal considered. She wanted nothing so much as a little peace and goodwill between them. But she knew Tanner had it right. DeDe was testing her, and she dare not fail or the situation was only going to get worse. "After you finish clearing off the table, bring me your homework. Then we'll see."

"Oh, fine. Just fine."

Crystal gritted her teeth and let the sarcasm pass.

Holding the line was one thing, but she had to be careful to choose the right battles.

After the meal, DeDe trotted out the homework. With great relief, Crystal saw that it all looked in order. She gave DeDe back her things.

"Thanks." The child actually managed to speak without rancor. She asked hopefully, "And tomorrow am I done being grounded?"

Crystal gave her a warm smile. "Yes. That's the plan."

"Okay." The child returned to her room and shut the door quietly.

Tanner waited in the kitchen after DeDe was in bed. He didn't have to wait long. Crystal appeared dressed for bed, same as the night before.

She didn't seem the least surprised to find him there. "Beer?"

He gave a single shake of his head. "I'll pass."

She put on the water for that tea she liked and then took the chair next to him. Bracing an elbow on the table, she cradled her chin on her hand. "You're looking very serious."

He wanted to kiss her. He wanted it bad. He sat back in his chair to make it easier not to reach for her. "Feeling okay?"

She grinned. "If you mean, am I about to chuck my supper in your lap, relax. I'm fine. Truly."

"Good." It came out sounding gruff. She got to him, always had. Until two nights ago, he'd told himself it was just the sex thing. But now, with the baby coming...

He needed to take care of her. To keep her safe. To make a place for her, a permanent one, in his life.

All that scared the crap out of him.

She was like some butterfly—so beautiful, soaring into his life on bright wings. Too bad about butterflies: They were here and then gone. The steady, solid woman he'd always thought he would marry would have been better. He knew that.

But now there was no turning back. Crystal had his baby. They were bound, the two of them.

He just needed to get her to realize that. He was making progress but it wasn't easy, taking it slowly, giving her space to come around, to decide for herself that she would do what he wanted her to do.

"Tanner…"

"What?"

She mirrored his pose in her womanly way, dropping her hand flat on the table, sitting back away from him. "You seem so…intense tonight. Is something wrong?"

He played it off with a lazy shrug. "Not a thing."

She cleared her throat, a nervous sound. "Well. Good."

"It went better with DeDe tonight," he said.

"Yeah." She smiled and those caramel-brown eyes lit up. "I could almost dare to hope I'm making progress."

"You're doing great," he said, and meant it.

"Well. Maybe we'll have smooth sailing from now on." She made a scoffing sound. "I wish." And then she jumped to her feet and flitted over to the counter, where she got down the mug she liked and took one of those round teabags from a canister, got out the honey and a spoon.

He watched her, thinking of the job he wanted her to take, of the marriage proposal he intended for her to accept—in time, anyway. And of her family.

Her family, the Cunninghams, who lived in Roseville…

There was more to her story than she had told him. Over time, if he was patient, she might tell him the deepest secret, the one she'd kept back from him the night before.

Or maybe she wouldn't. Maybe he'd never know the worst, the thing that had driven her to run away, change her name, and never return. Till now.

And not really even now. She'd come as far as Sacramento. But she'd yet to travel those extra twenty-plus miles to see her parents again. Maybe she never would.

That seemed wrong to him. However rough her parents had been on her, at least they were *there*. At least they made a home for her and did the best they could for her. It was a lot more than Tanner or his sisters had ever had.

The pot started whistling. He watched her pour the steaming water over the bag.

When Crystal first came rolling into Sacramento and she and Kelly became instant best friends, he'd wanted to check into Crystal's background. Kelly had made him promise he wouldn't. She'd trusted Crystal absolutely, right off the bat. And she wasn't having her big brother poking his nose in her friend's private life.

Under protest, Tanner had promised, and he'd kept that promise.

But things were different now. Now there was a baby coming, and it was his responsibility to do all in his power to give his child the advantages he had never had. Shedding a little light on Crystal's past would help him understand her better. And he needed to understand her. He needed to work every angle available to him in order to give his child a solid chance at a real family to grow up in.

She carried her tea to the table and sat down again. "All right." She slanted him a look. "You're staring at me."

He glanced away. "Sorry."

"Tell me what's on your mind. Please. The suspense is killing me." Her voice was light. Gently teasing. It occurred to him that he'd come a long way with her in the past couple of days.

He relaxed a little. Trust wasn't built in a day, after all. He said, "You were sick today...."

Her brow furrowed. And then she let out a low chuckle. "Oh, Tanner. No. You're not worried, are you?" She glanced toward the dining room, as if making sure DeDe wasn't lurking there. And pitched her voice to a confidential level. "Honestly. Morning sickness is perfectly normal at this stage."

"I know. I remember. With DeDe, Kelly was sick a lot the first few months. She would only eat soda crackers and water until about noon."

"But then *after* noon, she ate anything that wasn't nailed down, am I right?"

He chuckled, remembering. "Pretty much."

"So you know, then, there's nothing to worry about."

"I know. But it did get me thinking."

"Uh-oh."

"I'm serious. You should have a doctor for this."

She sat up straighter. "I do. Or I will, as of Tuesday. I went in last week to get blood drawn so they can run the basic prenatal tests."

"Did you get the results?"

"I'll get them Tuesday."

"Do you have insurance?"

"I'm paid up for the rest of the month through Bandley and Schinker. After that, I can probably get COBRA, extend the insurance I've got already through the state, until I get something else." She caught her lower lip between her pretty white teeth. "It could be a problem to switch. Usually a new policy doesn't cover preexisting pregnancies."

"However it works out, I'll help."

"I know you will." She brushed her fingers across the back of his hand, causing longing to shiver within him. "I'm glad," she added softly.

That did it—her gentle tone, her tender expression. He turned his hand over and captured her wrist. "What time?"

It satisfied some primitive part of him to watch her mouth go soft, to hear the way her breath caught. "I…for what?"

He lifted her hand, and turned it, palm up. And then he pressed his lips to the tender, pale flesh at the inside of her wrist where the delicate blue veins ran close to the surface. Her hand was cool, her skin like the velvety petals of some rare flower. He kissed the fleshy pad at the base of her thumb. And then he let go, quickly, before he was tempted to do more. "The doctor's appointment Tuesday. What time?"

She cradled her hand against her breasts, as if his kiss had burned her. "Um. Ten-thirty."

"Let me take you."

She blinked. "Oh. Well. It's not necessary, really."

"I *want* to take you."

"Oh, Tanner…"

"Just say yes."

And after a moment, she did.

* * *

In Crystal's opinion, Monday was a minor miracle.

The entire day passed without DeDe acting up. The girl went to school, went to her ballet lesson, came home, set the table, ate dinner without saying one hostile word, did her homework, took her bath.

And went to bed.

Tanner was out working that evening—getting the goods on some bad-acting husband, or so he'd claimed—so Crystal had her evening tea in her room. She lay in bed with the TV on low, watching sitcoms and reading the want ads, finding nothing interesting.

Ugh—job hunting. The worst. She'd made several calls that day, and, while DeDe was at school, even spent the time signing up at a couple of temp agencies. The agencies hadn't been thrilled when they learned she was available only nine to three weekdays for the next two weeks, but they did take her application and told her they'd be calling if anything came up.

She had an interview for the following week with another law firm, which made her more than a little depressed. Even without the horniest attorney in the Central Valley as her boss, she wasn't exactly longing to get back into answering the phones and typing letters for some lawyer.

At some point, she must have snoozed, because she jolted awake at the tap on her door.

Dragging herself higher against the headboard, she answered groggily, "Yeah?"

Tanner stuck his head in. He got a look at her mussed hair and sleepy expression. "Sorry. The light was on and I heard the TV…." He started to withdraw.

"Wait." The word slipped out before she could think of all the reasons she shouldn't be inviting him into her room in the middle of the night. But so what? She wanted a few minutes with him. Nothing wrong with that.

He pushed the door open enough to slip through and came and sat on the edge of the bed. The newspaper made soft crackling sounds as the bed shifted under his weight.

"So," he said softly. "Want ads putting you right to sleep?"

"Um."

"Forget those. Come and work for me."

"Just seeing what's available."

He shook his head. "Bad idea. Not to mention completely unnecessary." He smelled tempting as always—and also faintly of something green and outdoorsy.

That made her smile. "Been lurking in the bushes somewhere, taking pictures of a straying husband?"

He pretended to look threatening and growled, "It was a top-secret assignment."

"I'll bet."

And then he shrugged. "You're right. I *was* lurking in the bushes, snapping a few really incriminating candid shots. How did you guess?"

"You smell like geraniums. Fresh and green."

He picked up the remote and tipped his head at the TV. "You watching this?" When she shook her head, he pushed a button. The big screen went dark. "DeDe make it through the evening without pitching any fits?"

"She did." Her gaze strayed to his mouth. She wanted to feel his lips on hers. They would be cool, those lips. At first. But they would quickly grow warm....

He spoke again, his voice suddenly rough and wonderfully intimate. "You shouldn't look at me like that. Not unless you're about to tell me to lock the bedroom door and take off all my clothes…"

She shut her eyes. "You're right. I shouldn't. I'm sorry…."

His cool mouth touched hers. With a sigh, she responded, lifting a lazy hand, wrapping her fingers around his strong neck. Just as she'd known they would, his lips grew warm.

He was the one who broke the kiss.

She opened her eyes. "See that chair in the corner?"

He glanced over his shoulder. "It's a long way away."

"Go sit in it. Please."

"You're sure?"

"Unfortunately, yes."

He stood. She longed only to call him back down to her. But she controlled herself. Barely.

Once in the chair, he made himself comfortable, sticking his booted feet out in front of him, crossing them at the ankles. "Now what?"

"We make ordinary, everyday conversation."

"Well, all right." He seemed to think for a moment and then asked, "So since you just *have* to look around for a job when I've already given you one— having any luck?"

Tenderness moved through her, in a warm wave. He was so gorgeous and sexy and…good.

Yes. He was. He was good to her. Whatever happened, she knew he would be there for her. And for their child.

She'd never been a woman who made careful choices. She'd blown it, often. In the worst kinds of ways.

But Tanner Bravo…

Every day she was more certain that she couldn't have chosen a better father for the baby sleeping within her.

"Keep looking at me that way," he muttered. "I'll be back in that bed with you so fast…"

She picked up the paper, folded it in half and then in half again and tossed it off the side of the bed. "The job market sucks. I'm thinking maybe I'll have to work for you, after all."

Dark eyes went velvet black. "You're hired."

DeDe had another good morning. She was chatty and friendly at breakfast. Crystal found herself almost daring to hope that the demon child was no more, that sweet Deirdre was back to stay.

Once the nine-year-old was out the door, Tanner led Crystal into his temporary bedroom in the entry hall and handed her a set of keys and a scrap of paper. The paper had a Rancho Cordova address and a four-number alarm code on it. "The office is yours. You remember how to get there?"

She beamed at him. "How could I ever forget?" He also produced a check for twelve hundred dollars. She folded her arms over her chest and shook her head. "There is absolutely no need to pay me upfront."

He just stood there, holding it out. "Yeah. There is. You need the money and I want you to have it. I know you'll do a great job, so it's cash well spent."

"But I—"

"No buts. Take the check."

And she thought, why not? He was right, after all. She

would do a great job. And whether he paid her now or later, the amount would be the same. She held out her hand.

He muttered as he put the money in it, "I've never met a woman with so damned much integrity when it comes to money."

"Is that a criticism?" She slipped the check into a pocket. She'd get it into the bank that afternoon.

"Well, it's just that you're so big on taking life as it comes."

She laughed. "Oh. You think I ought to take money as it comes, too?"

"Well, why not?"

"Simple. Too dangerous. Debts weigh a person down. They inhibit the natural flow of good feelings and positive energy."

"So does being broke, if you think about it."

"True," she answered cheerfully. "But since being broke is a state of mind, I never have a problem with that."

He put up a hand, like a witness swearing an oath. "I give. Keep your integrity."

"Thank you, I will."

He glanced at his watch, which had a thick black band and all kinds of interesting dials and buttons on it. "Two hours till we have to be at the doctor's."

She did like the way he said *we.* "I think I'll go over to the office, have a look around, measure the windows for curtains."

He swore low. "There will be curtains?"

"Relax. Very masculine-looking curtains, I promise. And some manly throw pillows. All in colors other than brown."

"Crystal."

"What?"

"There is no such thing as a manly throw pillow."

"Watch. Learn. We'll also need a few plants. Maybe a ficus tree and a couple of hardy succulents."

"Hardy succulents," he repeated. He was shaking his head.

"I can do all this cheap, I swear. And don't worry. I do understand that the decor isn't the job."

"Whew."

"I need a computer."

"You can have the one in my office. I've got another PC at the house, along with a laptop."

"Okay. That's good. I want to go through the file cabinets in your office—and maybe move them up to the front area. And do you have an account with the bottled water people?" At his nod, she said, "Good. I'll call them, get them delivering again."

He teased, "And all that before ten-thirty."

"Not quite. But I can get started. And when you have some free hours to give me, we need to go over your accounts and the programs you use. It's my plan to be up and running, behind that desk, answering that phone when it rings, by the end of the week."

"You're making me tired, you know that?"

She only smiled. "You want to meet me there, at the office, at ten? We can drive to the OB-GYN's together."

"I've got nothing going on today until after noon. Why don't I just take you to the office now? Any questions you have, I'm there to answer."

"Great. But I need my car for later. I'll follow you." She turned for the door, in a hurry to get going, to get started on the grand adventure that was going to be her new job.

But Tanner caught her arm and pulled her back. "Slow down a minute…." He pulled her closer, up tight against his chest.

Her pulse beat a little faster and there was that sudden, delicious weakness in the region of her knees. And not only that; she also felt that melting sensation low in her midsection.

She looked up into those beautiful dark eyes of his. "Come *on*. Time's wasting."

"Oh, yeah." He lowered his mouth and she lifted hers to meet it, sliding her arms up the hard contours of his chest and clasping them around the back of his neck, running her eager fingers up into his thick hair.

She pulled back first—regretfully. "Tanner. I mean it. We have to go."

At the office they got the windows measured for the curtains, moved the computer up to the front desk, called to get the bottled water delivered again and Tanner showed Crystal a little of how he kept track of his accounts.

She learned that he'd built up his business over the years, mostly by word of mouth. He had a lot more clients than he could handle on his own. For the overflow, he hired other P.I.'s, independent contractors. He said that was when he'd really started to make money, when his business got big enough that he had to subcontract a good portion of it.

She whistled when confronted with his bottom line. "I am impressed. You must have a very nice nest egg."

"As a matter of fact, I do. Being broke interferes with my flow."

She faked a scowl. "It's not nice to mock the mother of your child."

"I was teasing, not mocking." He said it so…fondly.

And she looked into his eyes and thought about falling. Because she was.

She was falling for Tanner Bravo.

Falling for Tanner…

She was learning that what she felt for him was…more.

More than just sex, as amazing as sex could be with him. More, even, than the huge reality of having his baby.

What was happening here? Crystal didn't do the forever type of commitment. She honestly believed that kind of thing wasn't for her. She liked her life free and unencumbered.

But then again, she *was* having a baby. And keeping it. And that was a pretty enormous commitment. Maybe it wasn't all that surprising that suddenly she found herself considering the possibility of giving forever a chance.

Forever with Tanner. What next?

Love.

The word kind of snuck into her mind. Could it be? Really?

They'd been so careful, all along, never to say the word that starts with *L*. Tanner hadn't said it, even when he got after her to be open to the idea of marriage.

Love.

Oh, God. Having his baby. And now *this*….

Chapter Eight

At Dr. Louise Daniel's office, Tanner sat patiently beside Crystal in the waiting room as she filled out endless pages of paperwork. She lied on the health questionnaire and felt the usual twinge of guilt over it.

But then she reminded herself that it was *her* history to rewrite—or rather, the history of poor, screwed-up Martha Cunningham. And if it ever became necessary for the sake of the new life within her, she'd tell Dr. Daniel the truth and the whole truth, so help her God.

Pen poised at that crucial spot on the medical form, she sent the man beside her an oblique glance. He was thumbing through a dog-eared copy of *Time* magazine and didn't see her look his way.

Love. She thought the word again.

Love meant trust.

And soon, if they kept on the way they were going, she would have to tell him the rest of Martha's sad story. Her stomach twisted at the thought. The old pain for all she'd lost once was suddenly rising again, the old questions rolling over her like the raging waters of a flood.

Or a tsunami.

She willed the flood of pain and unanswered questions away. And she finished filling out the forms.

When the nurse called her name, Tanner said, "Beside the exam, there'll be a separate consultation, won't there?"

"I think so. You want to be there for that?"

"Yeah."

"I'll have them come get you," she promised, while inside a little curl of dread unfurled. She just wasn't ready to talk about the hardest things with him. Not yet.

But it *could* all come out now. It was possible the doctor would recognize the signs. Wasn't it?

Whatever. She had promised him he could be there to talk to the doctor. She asked the nurse, "When is the consultation?"

"Dr. Daniel likes to hold it after the exam."

"The baby's father came in with me. His name's Tanner Bravo. He wants to be in on the consultation, if that's all right."

"No problem. I'll see his included."

So it was arranged. He would be there to hear whatever the doctor had to say.

In the exam room, after the inevitable moments with her feet in the oven mitt-covered stirrups, Dr. Daniel studied her chart.

"First pregnancy…" the doctor said in a thoughtful tone.

Crystal said nothing. She sat utterly still on the exam table, waiting for the crucial question.

It never came.

A gentle hand touched her shoulder. "Go ahead and get dressed. We'll meet in my consultation room."

Tanner joined her in the small, bright room. They sat together facing a cherrywood desk. The walls were covered with framed snapshots of proud parents showing off bundled-up, squinty-face babies, no doubt children the doctor had delivered.

Tanner caught her hand. "You okay?"

"Great." And her heart lifted in spite of the lead weight low in her belly. If only there had been a guy like Tanner before.

But there hadn't. Far from it.

Tanner was frowning. "You look…not right. Scared, I think. Is something wrong?"

She brought their joined hands to her lips and kissed the back of his wrist, which was dusted with soft dark hairs. "No. Don't worry. Everything is fine."

Dr. Daniel bustled in carrying a sheaf of papers. She introduced herself to Tanner, took her seat behind the desk and laid the papers on her desk pad. At Crystal, she beamed a bright smile. "It's official. You are nine weeks pregnant. Everything is looking good. Your due date is December fourteenth." Sagittarius, Crystal thought. Tactless, quick-witted, honest, optimistic… She smiled to herself at the thought of her baby's possible sun sign. Of course, if the birth occurred a week later, he or she would be a Capricorn: gentle, receptive and enduring.

Not that it mattered what sun sign her child was born

under. He or she would be beautiful. And loved. And encouraged to live life fully, with joy…

Dr. Daniel had more to say. She talked about the basic stuff: eating a healthy diet with lots of fruits and veggies and making sure to get plenty of sleep. She advised moderate exercise and told Crystal that morning sickness was normal and so was frequent urination and tenderness of the breasts. She said the results of her lab work from the week before were looking good and she wanted to see her again in a month. Finally, she scribbled a prescription for prenatal vitamins. She held it out across the desk and Crystal took it.

"All right then," said the doctor. "Do either of you have any questions?"

Tanner said, "Not as long as you're telling us she's healthy and the baby is fine?"

The doctor nodded. "That is exactly what I'm telling you." She turned to Crystal again. "Get your sleep and avoid stress as much as possible. Eat right and take your vitamins. And sometime around December fourteenth, you'll be giving birth to a healthy newborn."

And that was it. They were dismissed. Ten minutes later, they were on their way back to the office. Crystal felt relief—and not only that the tiny life within her was healthy and doing well. If Dr. Daniel knew the truth, she'd seen no necessity to discuss it right then.

Which was good. Perfect. Before her next appointment, Crystal would sit down with Tanner and tell him everything—the hardest, most painful truth. The truth that, up till now, had been nobody's business but hers.

They stopped and got sandwiches and shared lunch at the office. Then he left for his appointment, and she went to the bank to deposit her check. After the bank, she shopped. She bought pillows and fabric.

Since Alicia Dean's mother was driving DeDe and her friends to their tap lesson after school, and then Lindsay's mom was taking the girls home, Crystal had until five before she had to be back at the house. She made use of the extra time, stopping at a local nursery to pick out some large, hardy plants, taking them back to the office and arranging them in the reception area.

And then there were a few things to pick up at Raley's. She got home at four forty-five. She was just trying to decide what to put together for dinner when the phone rang.

She grabbed the cordless off the table. "Hello?"

"Hi. Is this Crystal?" The voice on the other end had a slight tremor to it—of nerves? Of…fear? "You're taking care of DeDe while Kelly and Mitch are away?"

"I'm the one."

"This is Betty Carroll."

The name was familiar. Crystal checked the phone list on the fridge. "Lindsay's mom. Of course. You're bringing the girls home today."

Betty cleared her throat. "Yes. That's right. And I'm sorry, but there's a problem."

Crystal's mouth went dry. "Excuse me?"

"All the girls are here, at the studio, ready to go. Except Deirdre. I've sent the other girls to look for her—in the studio and up and down the street. They came back without her. Nobody seems to know where she's gone off to. I don't know what to do next. She's just disappeared."

Chapter Nine

Crystal sank, weak-kneed, to a chair.

Cisco, sensing her distress, rose from his spot in the corner and came over to sit at her side. Absently, she gave the dog a pat on the head and tried to think clearly.

DeDe vanished.

Impossible. No way...

She struggled to push back the paralyzing fog of fear and denial, to ask the right questions of the worried woman on the other end of the line. "The girls checked the bathrooms? And are you sure she isn't waiting out by your car?"

"Honestly. We've checked everywhere, including the bathrooms and out by the car. *Everywhere...*"

"What about the woman at the front desk?"

"I just talked to her. She says she didn't see her go out."

"And the tap teacher?"

"Same thing. She hasn't seen DeDe since she dismissed the class."

Crystal's mind was a blank landscape of pure panic for the troubled little girl. "What about the other girls? Did they say she was…okay the last time they saw her?"

A pause, then, "They didn't mention a problem. But I didn't ask them. I'll talk to them."

"Thank you. And…could you wait there, at the studio? I'll be there in fifteen minutes."

"Of course. We'll be here."

"Here's my cell number." She rattled it off. "Call me if she appears."

"Absolutely."

Crystal hung up, grabbed her purse and her cell and headed for the door. She was halfway down the front walk, her cell to her ear after autodialing Tanner, when she saw the black Mustang turn the corner, coming her way.

He pulled into the driveway next to her Camaro and rolled the window down. "You're white as a sheet. What's wrong?"

"Thank God you're here."

"Is it the baby?" He started to get out.

"No don't. We have to go, now…."

He sank back into the seat. "Where? Are you sick?"

"No, it's not the baby. I'm okay." She put her cell in her bag as she raced around the front of her car to the passenger side of his. Yanking the door wide, she dropped into the seat and reached for the seat belt.

"Crystal. What the hell is happening here?"

"It's DeDe." She hauled the door shut and then hooked the belt. "Lindsay's mom came to pick her up at the dance studio—and somehow, she's disappeared. Sometime after the lesson was over, Lindsay's mom said. I was just going over there."

Without another word, Tanner put it in reverse. The car shot backward into the street.

On the way to the studio, she filled him in on what she knew, which wasn't much.

A stocky brunette and four scared-looking girls were waiting in the reception area when Crystal and Tanner walked in. Crystal had met all four children at one time or another. They were Alicia and Mia and Lindsay and Devon Marie.

The woman, Betty, jumped up. "Crystal?"

"Yes. And this is Tanner, DeDe's uncle."

Betty nodded at Tanner—and then shook her head. "No sign of her yet." She glanced back at the miserable-looking row of girls. "Devon Marie."

A pretty child with short, black curls rose reluctantly and approached. "I'm sorry. So sorry. I didn't mean it..."

Betty put a hand on her small shoulder to steady her. "This is DeDe's uncle Tanner and Crystal."

"I know them," said the child. "Hi..." She tried a smile but didn't quite make it.

Betty squeezed her shoulder. "You need to tell them what you told me."

Tears welled in the little girl's eyes. "I didn't mean to hurt her feelings. I only..."

Tanner spoke gently. "Devon Marie. You can help a lot by just telling us what happened."

"I...okay."

"Go ahead," said Crystal. "Please."

"Um, well, it was right after tap class. We were all

walking to the dressing room to get our packs, you know, and shoes. I was talking about our new pool at my house and how it will be finished by the Fourth of July and how I would have a pool party for everyone then. And DeDe said how *she* was going to have a party on the Fourth of July at *her* pool and I couldn't have one if she was going to have one…" Devon Marie made a sniffling sound as the tears spilled over and trailed down her round cheeks.

Betty produced a tissue. The girl took it, wadded it in a ball and dabbed at her eyes.

Betty said, "Go ahead, honey. Tell the rest. It's okay."

Devon Marie stifled a sob. "I…I wanted to have the party at my new pool and I felt kinda mad at DeDe, so I said, 'Well, you'll probably be moved away by the Fourth of July, so what do you care?' And DeDe didn't say anything. But her face got really red. We were going by the bathroom then. She turned and went in there, hitting the door hard to push it open. I was going to go in there and say sorry…" She cast a sad little glance back at her seated friends.

Mia Lu, a slim little Asian girl with straight dark hair pulled into two high ponytails, spoke up then. "She *was* going to go in there. But I told her to wait and maybe in a few minutes DeDe wouldn't be so mad."

Devon Marie swiped at her eyes and swallowed yet another sob. "And we just kept going to the dressing room—oh, I should have gone in there with her, no matter how mad she was. I should have said sorry. It's all my fault…"

"Oh, honey," said Betty. "Honey, don't cry…"

Crystal tried to soothe her, too. "Sometimes friends

get in arguments. We're going to find her now." *Please God. Let us find her.* "And later, you two can make up. Okay?"

Dark curls bounced as Devon Marie nodded. "Okay…"

"What else can we do?" Betty asked.

Tanner said, "Go ahead and take the girls home for now."

"We'll call," Crystal promised, "the minute we know anything."

Once Betty and the girls were gone, Tanner talked to the receptionist. The woman said there was another exit besides the main one, but an alarm buzzed if anyone tried to use it. She admitted she'd been in the back room, through the door behind the reception desk, around the time the tap class got out. It was possible that Deirdre had slipped by her.

"We should have a look around," Tanner said. He asked for directions to the room upstairs where DeDe had had her lesson.

From there, he and Crystal retraced the child's steps, down a hallway, back down the stairs. They checked in corners and down adjacent hallways. They opened any door they came to, asked people passing by if they'd seen a girl fitting DeDe's description in the past forty-five minutes. No one had.

Tanner had Crystal look around the girl's bathroom. She found nothing to signal that DeDe had even been there. They headed for the dressing room. Crystal went in. DeDe's pack, with her school things and her street shoes, hung on a lonely peg in there.

She took it out to Tanner.

"So wherever she is," he said. "She's in tap shoes."

"You'd think people would hear her coming."

He was frowning. "I don't think she's still in the studio."

"Why not?"

"Instinct, partly. Which isn't always reliable. But as far as we know, since she ducked into the restroom, no one has seen her. She never went and collected her pack. She was mad, right?"

"Sure sounds like it."

"I see her taking off."

Anxiety had Crystal's stomach roiling. Just what she needed right now. Another bout of morning sickness. She pressed her hand to her belly and willed the nausea away. "Maybe we should call Kelly and Mitch…."

He wrapped an arm around her, steadying her. "We might have to." And the police. She knew he was thinking it, too. "But not yet," he said. "First we'll try seeing if she decided to walk home."

"But Tanner, we didn't see her on the way here…"

"There's more than one way to get here."

"But if she went home, one of us should be there."

"On foot, that would take her a while—plus, she has a key, right?" He waited for her nod. "I don't think there's any need to rush back to the house. Come on. Let's go."

On the way out, Crystal gave the receptionist her cell number. The woman promised to call immediately if DeDe appeared or anyone came by with information about her.

They got in the Mustang and started driving—up one street and down another. For twenty minutes, they scoured the area around Madame Arletty's Dance Academy in a slowly widening grid.

Twice, Crystal dialed the house. All she got was the answering machine.

Her heart beat a sick tattoo in her chest, and her stomach kept on churning. Silently she prayed, *Please, please. Let her be all right. Please keep her safe. Please let us find her, now...*

It didn't happen. They kept turning corners onto new streets, with no sign of an angry brown-haired girl in a leotard, shorts and tap shoes.

Finally Tanner glanced across at her.

She read his thoughts in his bleak expression. "It's not happening, is it?"

He shook his head and turned his gaze to the street ahead again. "We'll go back to Kelly's. Take it from there."

Take it from there? Meaning call the police—and Mitch and Kelly? Oh, God. Where *was* she? *Please, please, let her be safe....*

Crystal swallowed the lump of fear in her throat. "Yeah. Let's go." The words came out in a half-whisper, since her throat had clutched up tight again.

He turned right at the next corner, and then left and right again—and they were back on the regular route between the academy and Kelly's house. The May sun shone down and traffic was a bear and it seemed like such an ordinary day.

How could DeDe go missing on a day like this? It should be dark out, the sky black with threatening clouds. There should be hard, bright lightning. And high winds and driving rain...

Crystal stared out the windshield at the sunshiny day and took careful breaths through her nose in an effort to avoid having to ask Tanner to stop. She didn't have time to lose her lunch right now. Right now, DeDe was missing and needed to be found.

She shut her eyes, breathed some more through her nose, prayed, *Please. Bring her home safe. Please...*

And when she looked again, her prayer was answered. A hundred yards ahead, striding fast along the sidewalk, she saw the girl in the electric-green leotard and purple tap shorts. She saw the sun glint off a swinging swatch of long tan hair. "Tanner! Oh, God. She's there." Crystal pointed.

He swore and expertly maneuvered the car into the right lane. "At last," he said low.

She couldn't have agreed with him more.

In seconds they caught up to DeDe. The car crawled along the curb beside her. Crystal rolled down the window.

DeDe, taps click-clicking fast along the pavement, chin set and mouth tight, cast a nervous glance toward the car. When she saw who it was, she stopped stock-still and put her hand to her mouth.

Then she burst into tears.

Chapter Ten

Crystal barely got the car door open before fifty pounds of nine-year-old landed in her arms.

There were no words. DeDe sobbed her young heart out, and Crystal held on tight, gladness and relief pouring through her like a cool stream of clear water, thinking of all the poor, lost children in the world. She knew that DeDe was still lost, in her heart.

But the rest of her was right here, in Crystal's cherishing arms. For now, that had to be enough.

The storm of weeping passed as abruptly as it had started. DeDe pulled away. "I left my pack. I just walked out."

Crystal gestured at the backseat where the pack waited. "We got it."

She turned and flipped the seat down. DeDe climbed

in. Crystal got in, too, handed DeDe a Kleenex over the seat and buckled up.

Tanner eased the Mustang away from the curb and into the thick flow of afternoon traffic.

During the ride back Crystal called Betty and the receptionist at the academy to tell them DeDe was safe and unhurt. Betty promised to tell the girls their friend had been found.

When they reached the house, DeDe went straight to her room.

Tanner and Crystal stood in the hallway near the front door, listening to DeDe's door closing, to the tap-tap of Cisco's doggy nails on the hardwood floor, his soft whine when he reached DeDe's shut door. They heard her let him in.

And then there was silence.

She swayed toward him and he wrapped an arm around her.

Her head felt as heavy as the rest of her, suddenly. She rested it on his strong shoulder. "It's like after some horrible explosion."

"Yeah." He grunted, pressed his warm lips to the top of her head. "My ears are still ringing…."

"Dear God. My legs are shaking."

"Come on…" The door to his temporary bedroom was right there. They went in and shut the door. He guided her over to the daybed.

She dropped onto it with a grateful sigh and he came down beside her. "So," she said wearily. "What now? Should we go talk to her?"

He nodded. "The poor kid…" And his voice trailed off.

So they went to DeDe's door together. He gave it a tap. Crystal said, "DeDe?"

And the door swung open. "Please," DeDe said in a tiny voice. "Can I just be by myself now?"

"Honey," said Crystal, "we have to talk about this."

Tanner said, "That was a dangerous move you made, running off like that. Anything could have happened to you. You scared us. Bad. We were so worried about you."

"Please," the little girl said again, her small chin trembling. "Just for a little while, can you leave me alone?"

"No," Tanner told her. "I don't think we can."

A tear spilled over DeDe's cheek, but she did step clear of the door. The adults went in. Tanner stood by the window and Crystal sat on the bed.

DeDe dropped down beside her—but not too close. "Okay. I'm sorry. It was a bad thing to do. I just got so mad and I…" She seemed to run out of words.

Crystal spoke quietly. "We have to call your parents about this. It's very likely they'll decide to come home."

DeDe made a sound of real distress. "I don't want to ruin their trip. I really don't. I know I was terrible when they left. I feel bad about it. I feel bad about everything lately. But I…oh, I don't know. I just don't know…." She hung her head. The tears were falling again. Tanner yanked a few tissues from the box on the dresser and gave them to her. She blew her nose and dabbed her eyes. "Did Devon Marie tell you what I got mad about?"

"She did." Crystal repeated what the other child had said. "Is that what happened?"

DeDe nodded. "That's right." And then she was shaking her lowered head. "I just…well, I *always* have the Fourth of July party. And now *she* wants to have it.

And probably she'll always have it and I won't even be here anymore…."

Crystal couldn't stop herself. She tried to reach out.

But DeDe only shrugged her off. "Please. Can I just be by myself now?"

Crystal and Tanner shared a look. Tanner shrugged.

"We're right here," said Crystal. "If you need us…."

Tanner led the way out the door. They went to the kitchen, for lack of anywhere better to go, and sat at the table.

Crystal pressed her fingers to the tender skin beneath her eyes. "What time is it where Kelly and Mitch are?"

He pushed a button on his watch. "A little after five in the morning."

She groaned. "This call is going to upset them enough—I hate to scare them to death waking them up before dawn."

He shrugged. "I suppose we can wait a few hours, at least until they're out of bed…."

"You think?"

"Yeah. Unless DeDe says she needs to talk to them, seems like it should be okay."

"All right then. We'll call right before she goes to bed…unless she wants it otherwise."

"Fine." He rested his arms on the table, hung his dark head let out a humorless laugh.

"What?" she asked.

He turned his head and their eyes met. "I had this bright idea of how great it would be, to practice being married while Mitch and Kelly are gone. I thought how we'd even have a kid to take care of, how we would work together looking after DeDe…."

She chuckled, too, then. "Look at it this way. We *are* working together."

He gave her a wry thumbs-up. "Doing the best we can with the hand we've been dealt."

"Like most parents, I guess…" She thought of her own father, then, which she generally tried not to do. Dickson Cunningham had been a terrible dad, rigid and uncompromising. And always angry in a quiet, controlled, seething kind of way. He only got angrier the more trouble she made. By the end, she had sworn that she hated him. She'd been certain he hated her right back.

Now, though, with the perspective of years and a little maturity, she couldn't help but wonder how much her flailing wild-child self had hurt him. How much he had suffered and worried for her…

Tanner reached out, brushed a hand down the side of her face. "Hey. Still with me?"

She smiled. "Just thinking of my father, of all things. I hated him. I really did. I only saw how he didn't understand me. How he wanted me to be someone I could never be. How he…" She let the sentence die unfinished.

"How he what?" Tanner's eyes were watchful.

She remembered the promise she'd made to herself in Dr. Daniel's office that morning, to tell him the hardest truth. She *would* keep that promise. Soon.

He prompted again, "You remember how your father, what?"

"How he yelled at me all the time."

"And?"

"That's all."

"We both know that's not true."

So, she thought as she stared into those dark eyes of his. He knew she wasn't telling him everything. She wasn't surprised. He was, after all, a P.I. It was his nature, ingrained in him, to sense people's secrets, to go after the truth.

Too bad. This was *her* truth. And he would have to trust her enough to wait until she was ready to share it with him.

She gave him a tired shrug. "You're right. There's more. But I'm not up for going into it now."

"If there's anything I can—"

She put a finger against those fine lips of his. "I know. Thank you. At the moment, though, we have other things we have to deal with. Now, it's about DeDe."

He glanced away—but then he faced her again. "Yeah. You're right."

"And until we make that call to Mitch and Kelly, I'm thinking we'll carry on as usual. Dinner. Homework. Evening news."

"Makes sense to me."

She asked, "Do you need to go back to work tonight?"

"Yeah. I've got a few loose ends I ought to tie up. I was going to deal with them after dinner, but I'm thinking I should be here when you make that call."

"I would appreciate it."

He rose. "So I'm outta here. I'll be back by eight or so. Save me some leftovers."

"You know I will."

So he took off and Crystal cooked dinner. When it was just about ready, she went to get DeDe.

DeDe answered quickly at Crystal's knock. She'd changed into jeans and a T-shirt. Her eyes were huge and solemn.

"How are you doing?" Crystal asked gently.

"Okay."

"Come and set the table?"

"Sure."

Crystal turned without saying more. She heard DeDe and the dog fall in behind her. In the kitchen, Cisco went to his corner.

"Will Uncle Tanner be here?"

"No. He has to work. Just set it for the two of us."

DeDe got the placemats from the drawer and counted out the few pieces of flatware. She put the plates on, folded two paper napkins into neat triangles and put the forks on top of them. She went to get the glasses. "Are you having milk?"

"Yes, thank you. And you can go ahead and pour it."

DeDe poured and Crystal put the food on the table. They sat down, spread their paper napkins on their laps.

Crystal passed her the salad. DeDe took the bowl and then set it down. "Crystal?"

"Uh-huh?"

"Am I grounded?"

"Do you think you *should* be grounded?"

A silence. An extended one. Finally, "Oh, well. Yeah. I guess. For how long?"

"I think your parents will decide that."

"When will you call them?"

"Before you go to bed."

"Will they come home, you think?"

"Do you want them to?"

DeDe pressed her lips together, contrite. "I…no. I don't. It wouldn't be right."

"Honey, I honestly can't say what they'll decide. I can't speak for them."

"I know…"

"Come on, now. Take your salad."

DeDe picked up the salad tongs and transferred the greens to her wooden salad bowl. Crystal passed her the platter of chicken kabobs. DeDe took one. There was rice. She took a spoonful of that, too. And then she picked up her fork—and set it back down again. "I just got…so mad. I hid in the bathroom. I went in one of the toilet stalls and shut the door and just stood there, staring at the stall door, thinking that if Devon Marie came in there after me, I would tell her that I hated her."

Crystal asked softly. "And do you hate her? Do you hate your friend?"

"She said—"

"I know what she said. And you didn't answer my question. Do you hate your friend?"

"No. No, I don't hate her. I just *felt* like I did then. Because I was so mad."

"Just like when you said that you hated your dad. Because you were mad."

DeDe looked at her suspiciously. "Yeah. So?"

"And how's all this working out for you?"

The child gazed miserably down at her rice and kabob. "Okay. It's not so good."

"There's an old saying, You can't unring that bell. You know what it means?"

DeDe stared harder at her plate. "No."

"Well, a bell rings. You can't take that sound back. You can never make it so that bell didn't ring. Just like when you say something really hurtful to someone, something you maybe didn't even mean."

DeDe glanced up. "Like 'I hate you'?"

"Exactly. If you tell someone you hate them, they will always remember you said that. You can't make them forget. All you can do is show them over and over that you didn't mean it, that you do care for them, that you hold them in high regard and that you've learned not to say hurtful things you don't really mean."

"But I didn't say 'I hate you' to Devon Marie."

"And isn't that great?"

"Huh?"

"It's one bell you don't have to wish you could unring. But you did run away today."

"I was only going home."

"Uh-uh. That's no excuse. You ran away from your friends, and you weren't there to ride home with Mrs. Carroll, as everyone was counting on you to be. You had us all terrified that something awful could have happened to you. Poor Devon Marie cried. She felt so bad about the argument you had with her and was so worried that you might not be okay. That was one serious bell you rang today, and you know that it was."

DeDe met her eyes across the table. A single tear tracked a shining path down her cheek. "Crystal?"

"Yes?"

"Is it okay if we just eat now?"

Crystal picked up her fork. "It is. Absolutely."

* * *

After dinner, DeDe started to retreat to her room again.

Crystal, who thought the girl had spent enough time brooding alone, stopped her. "Stay out here. Keep me company."

"But I…"

"DeDe, do you want to call your mom and dad now? We can do that. It's okay."

DeDe shook her head. Hard. "No." It was clear she dreaded their reaction. "You said at bedtime. We can do it then."

"Sometimes it's better to get a difficult thing over with, you know?"

DeDe pressed her lips together. "Bedtime, okay? Please?" Now those lips were quivering.

"All right," Crystal said, then shamelessly bargained, "If you'll stop hiding in your room. Get a book and come on into the family room. Or forget the book if you want. Watch television with me."

DeDe agreed. She didn't even try making a play for the Disney Channel.

They were halfway through *Countdown* when the phone rang. It was Tanner. "I got a call on a meeting I wasn't expecting. I really should try and make this. I was going to be back by eight, but it'll be more like nine."

"It should be okay. We won't be calling Mitch and Kelly till nine-fifteen or so. I really would like you here for that, if at all possible."

"I'll be there. How's DeDe?"

"Fine. Right here with me. We're watching Keith Olbermann."

"Good. I was going to say we probably shouldn't let her mope in her room too much."

She glanced at the child sitting beside her on the couch. "Handled. You want to talk to her?"

"Sure."

"It's Tanner," Crystal said as she passed DeDe the phone.

"Hi," the little girl said. A series of one-word answers followed. "Yeah…okay…fine." She was far from her old, sparkling self, but at least she sounded interested in her uncle's questions. And her tone was pleasant enough. "I love you, too," she said at last and handed the phone back to Crystal.

"She sounds a little better than before," he said.

"Yeah, I think so.…"

"You sure you're okay on your own for a while longer?"

"I'm fine. Get here as soon as you can."

"You know I will."

She hung up and thought, as she had more than once recently, about how far the two of them had come in the past few days, how easy it was becoming to count on him, though most of her life she'd made it a point of honor to count on no one.

Love, she thought with a secret smile. Is this what love is?

To think of him with warmth and fondness, to look forward to their private times together. To want to turn to him with her problems, to know she could trust him completely…

The hotel bar was quiet and dimly lit, the bar itself a long, gleaming expanse of ebony, the mirrored wall behind stacked with shining bottles full of just about every liquor made.

Tanner took a black-clothed table in the corner, within sight of the entrance. He ordered a club soda. When it came, he sipped it slowly and watched the door.

A woman appeared. Around fifty. Blond. Tan pantsuit, a brown purse and good-quality brown shoes to match, all so plain as to be depressing. She glanced nervously around—at the bar, the tables…

When her gaze collided with Tanner's, he raised a hand.

She nodded, seemed to gather herself and started toward him. He rose to meet her.

"Tanner?" She had golden-brown eyes—Crystal's eyes, minus the lively shine.

"Mrs. Cunningham," he said. "Thank you for seeing me."

Chapter Eleven

Ann Cunningham ordered ginger ale. And then didn't touch it.

In her soft, sad voice she asked about her daughter. "Is she well?"

"Yes, she is. Very well."

"No…problems with drugs?"

"None." He said it firmly, remembering Crystal telling him about her growing-up years, how unhappy she'd been. And that there had been drugs. Crystal on drugs. Hard to imagine. He'd never seen her take more than a glass of wine now and then.

The woman across from him released a small, relieved sigh. "I've worried about that. There were drugs, when she was in her teens. Along with all the rest of it."

"The rest of it?"

She slanted him a wary look. "Yes," she said, and that was all. Her expression said she hadn't come here to speak of things that were none of his business.

Tanner didn't push. He had to watch himself. He wanted—*needed*—to know more than Crystal had told him. But he'd convinced this woman to talk to him by implying that Crystal had hired him. If she realized he was on his own with this, she might get up and walk out before he got any new information out of her.

He said, "Well, I can say for certain that she doesn't do drugs."

"...and she wants to see us?"

"Yeah. I think she does."

Ann looked at him sharply. "You *think?*"

"She's considering it."

"But...she sent you to talk to me, didn't she?"

He made a low noise that could have been interpreted to mean just about anything.

Crystal's mom accepted it as a yes. "I don't know..."

"About what?"

"My husband's been ill. Martha always upset him. He always said, when she left, that it was probably for the best."

Probably for the best to lose your daughter? Tanner's gut tightened. He didn't know what he'd expected exactly, but not this. Shouldn't a mother be grateful to hear she might be seeing her daughter again?

He thought of Crystal, her gorgeous smile, the light in her eyes, that quick mind and ready laugh, the bright colors she favored. Though she'd told him about her parents, said they were strict and uncompromising, he just couldn't imagine her with a sad, stiff mouse of a mother like this one.

The stiff mouse had stiffened even more. "Just a minute." The brown eyes were cold now, cold as black ice on a bad road in the middle of the night. "You're acting oddly, Tanner. And it's suddenly very clear to me why." He knew then she'd somehow figured out that Crystal hadn't hired him after all. But then she demanded, "It's about the child, isn't it?"

"The child," he repeated flatly. What child?

"Of course it is." Ann Cunningham looked like she'd sucked on a very sour lemon. "With Martha, it's always about the child."

The child? This woman knew about the baby? He couldn't see how. He certainly hadn't told her. And as far as he knew, Crys had yet to get in touch with her.

"The child?" he repeated—again—for lack of anything better to say.

Clutching her brown purse tightly, Ann Cunningham shot to her feet. "Tell my daughter what my husband and I have always told her. Giving the child up was the right thing to do. Martha was only sixteen—much too young to raise a child under any circumstances. And Martha had so many problems. She was not equipped to be a mother. The child went to a fine, Christian home. My husband and I personally saw to that. It was a closed adoption through a private agency. Martha has no right to disrupt the life of that child or her adopted family. Tell her she will never get any information out of me or her father. Tell her I will pray for her. And I hope that someday she will learn to move on."

* * *

On the drive back to Sacramento, Tanner took stock of what he'd learned.

How had the woman said it? *Martha has no right to disrupt the life of that child or* her *adopted family...*.

So then. Crystal had had a little girl once. And had given her up for adoption. *Closed* adoption—meaning she knew nothing about the family that had taken her baby and they knew nothing of her, aside from any medical information necessary for the sake of the child's health and well-being.

Now that he'd met Crystal's mother, he had no trouble picturing how it all happened.

Crystal, barely more than a kid herself, bullied into signing her child away. Her baby had been taken from her, and no one would tell her who the adoptive parents were.

Tanner sped along the freeway, lead-footing it a little, intent on making it back to the house before Crystal called Kelly and Mitch.

Guilt crept into the muscles at the back of his neck, drawing them tight. He should have waited. He knew that. Let her tell him in her own way, when she was ready. But sometimes he wondered if she would ever be ready.

What else had Ann Cunningham said? *Tell her she will never get any information out of me or her father...*.

There were other ways to find a child of a closed adoption. Tanner knew those ways.

Now that he'd learned this much, he had to find out more.

Crystal was starting to worry that Tanner wouldn't make it back in time for the all-important call to Kelly and Mitch. But he walked in the door at ten after nine.

She met him in the front hall. "Whew," she said. "I'm so glad you're here."

"Everything okay? DeDe…?"

"She's fine. Nervous about the phone call. She just finished her shower. I heard her go into her bedroom a minute or two ago. I was kind of thinking one of us should make the call and explain the situation. The other can sit with DeDe until Kelly and Mitch are ready to talk to her."

"Sounds good. You want me to handle the call?"

She shook her head. "Not unless you really want to. Technically, they left DeDe in my care…."

He touched her shoulder, a gesture of support and reassurance. "However you want it, that's fine with me."

"Well, okay then. I'll make the call. You be with DeDe."

"You got it."

Kelly answered the phone sounding drowsy and content. "Crystal. Hi."

"I woke you up. I'm sorry…."

"Hey. We weren't sleeping. Just lazing in bed. At home, we never get to sleep past seven." From nearby, Mitch said something. Kelly laughed. "Mitch says hi."

"Hi back. Um. Kelly, I…" Oh, boy. How to strike the right tone on this?

"What?" The drowsiness had vanished. Kelly was fully alert. "Something's wrong. Omigod. DeDe. Is she—"

"Kell. It's okay. She's perfectly fine, in her room at this moment, I promise you."

"What, then? Tell me."

"Today she ran away after her dance lesson."

Kelly gasped. "Ran away? Why?"

"She got mad at one of her friends and she stormed off—decided, without telling anyone, to walk home on her own."

"But she's safe? You found her."

"Yes. We found her. And she's safe." Crystal could hear Mitch in the background, demanding to know what the hell was happening.

Kelly said, "Just a minute…" And Crystal heard their voices, muffled, as Kelly filled him in. Finally, she came back on the line. "This is too scary. We're coming home."

"Whatever you think is best."

Kelly blew out a breath. "What do *you* think? Say it."

Crystal shook her head, though there was no one there to see. "Uh-uh. Not my call. You don't need the sitter telling you what to do."

"Crys. Damn it. You're there. We're not. Tell me what you think."

"Oh, Kell…"

"Tell me."

Crystal strove to get her thoughts in order. "Well, um…I think there are two ways to look at this—that she needs you and you'd better get back here, ASAP, or that this is something she should be allowed to work through, that maybe she's finally managed to scare even herself a little. Maybe in the long run, the last thing she needs is to know she ruined her parents' honeymoon."

Kelly added, "Or that all she has to do is misbehave and her mom and dad will come running home?"

Crystal made a low noise in her throat. "Really and truly, I just don't know…."

"How is she, I mean, how is she dealing with what she did?"

"She cried like a baby when we found her. After that, she's been…very quiet. Sad. And thoughtful, really."

"You think we should finish our honeymoon." It wasn't a question.

Crystal said, "No. Not going there. I told you what I think. If I were in your shoes, I might go either way."

"Sometimes I hate being a parent."

Crystal put a protective hand on her still-flat belly— and she thought, with deep sadness of her other baby. Her first child, eight years old now. A year younger than DeDe. Was she happy, with that fine, upstanding family she'd supposedly gone to? Was she well?

"Crys? Still there?"

Crystal sat a little straighter. "I'm here. And yes, I hear it's one tough job being a mom. But somebody's got to do it."

"You haven't said—what about you? Are you sick and tired of dealing with my troublesome daughter?"

"No." Crystal spoke firmly. "Not in the least. I love DeDe. She's a little confused these days, but she's still the greatest kid around. Under no circumstances are you to come home on my account. Understood?"

"Okay, then. Where's Tanner?"

"He's in the other room with DeDe. Shall I get him for you?"

Another hard sigh. "Tell you what. Let us talk to her first."

So Crystal took the phone to DeDe's room, where the child sat on the bed with Tanner. She was leaning against him and he had a protective arm wrapped around her.

DeDe stiffened and drew herself up when Crystal entered. Her eyes were wide and worried in her clean-scrubbed face.

"Your mom and dad want to talk to you." Crystal handed her the phone.

DeDe clutched it to her ear. "Mom? Oh, Mom…" And the tears started flowing.

Crystal sent Tanner a look. He rose. Together they went out of the room, gently closing the door behind them.

They went to the kitchen to wait. The minutes crawled by. For a time, they just sat there. Crystal took comfort in Tanner's presence at her side. She found it reassuring that he was there. It was good to know that if she reached out her hand, his would be waiting.

But he seemed a little agitated. He rose and stood by the sink and then went to the fridge, opened the door—and shut it without getting anything from inside.

She asked, "You okay?"

"Sorry," he said. He speared his fingers back through his dark hair and then glanced at his watch. "I should have gotten here sooner."

"Oh, stop. I told you I could handle it. Don't be hard on yourself because you had to work." He looked at her so strangely, then. A look of…what? Guilt? Concern? "Tanner? Are you okay? Is something going on here that I'm not getting?"

He stepped closer, reached down, framed her face in his two big hands.

She caught his wrists and sought an answer in his dark eyes. "What is it?"

He bent and brushed a kiss across her lips. "Nothing." His cradling hands dropped away. "Maybe we should check on her…"

She shook her head. "She'll bring the phone out here when they're done talking."

"You think they'll come home?"

She rose and put her hands on his shoulders. The powerful muscles there were bunched hard beneath her touch. "Will you relax?"

"I'm relaxed."

"Liar. Turn around."

"You don't have to—"

"Come on. Turn around."

He gave in and did as she instructed. She went to work, using thumbs, fingers and the pads of her hands to ease out the tension in his shoulders and back.

He let his head hang loose, and a pleasured groan escaped him. "Your hands are amazing, you know that?"

She worked her thumbs down the bumps of his spine. "It's all about energy points, getting to the places where the body stores tension and then working the muscles until the tension dissipates…." She rubbed. "There… and there. And what *have* you been doing this evening to get your back in such a state?"

"Long story…" He let out another groan. And then, across the dining room, on the other side of the house, they heard a door open.

Crystal ran the backs of her fingers up from the base of his spine, swift and sure, giving the tension a way to escape. And then she let her hands drop to her sides. He turned to face her again as DeDe came toward them carrying the phone. Her nose was red and her eyes swollen in the aftermath of tears.

He reached out a big hand and gathered her close to his side. "You doing okay?"

She ducked her head against him, kind of burrowing in. "Yeah. I guess…" He wrapped both arms around her, and she extended the phone to Crystal. "Mom and Dad need to talk to you again now."

Crystal put the phone to her ear. "Hi."

"Hey. Well, we've had a long talk and DeDe has promised to end the tantrums and bad behavior. She seems to mean it." Crystal gave the child, huddled close to her uncle, a fond glance. And Kelly went on, "So as of now, Mitch and I are continuing the honeymoon."

"Well, all right."

"We've come up with a plan for regular phone calls. She'll call us every other night before bed. That should give us a chance to talk about what's bothering her before it gets out of hand."

"And a chance to check for yourselves that she's doing all right."

"Exactly. She thinks she should be grounded. I don't really think grounding is going to matter much in this situation, but I do think she feels it's a way to make up for her actions. So fine. We'll call grounded and you can play that by ear."

"Will do."

"Good. Tanner there?"

"Right here." She handed him the phone.

When Kelly was done telling her brother what she'd told Crystal, DeDe asked for the phone again. She told her parents she loved them and said goodbye.

Then she glanced from her uncle to Crystal and softly suggested, "I would really like it if both of you would come and tuck me in."

So the three of them went to DeDe's room together. She climbed into bed and Tanner and Crystal each kissed her good-night.

"I will do better. I will," she vowed.

Crystal said, "We know you will," and turned off the light.

The next morning before school, Devon Marie called. DeDe took the call in her room.

At the table, Crystal pushed her half-finished bowl of oatmeal aside. "I hope they work things out between them."

Tanner reached across the table and put his hand over hers. "Don't worry. They're making up, not starting a fight all over again."

"You think?"

"Oh, yeah. Yesterday scared the crap out of both of them. I'd lay strong odds they're ready to compromise."

DeDe emerged ten minutes later wearing a smile. "Devon and me agreed. If I still live here on the Fourth of July, we'll have the party here. If I've moved away by then, we'll have it at her house."

Tanner swallowed a big bite of scrambled eggs. "Sounds like a good plan to me."

"Yes," said DeDe, as she pulled a carton of orange juice from the fridge. "Things are going to be different soon. But I can still come and see my old friends sometimes. And I will also make new ones."

Crystal said, "That's right. The move is going to mean that you'll make even more friends."

Tanner grunted in agreement and sipped his coffee.

DeDe carried her glass to the table. "Devon Marie is having a sleepover Saturday night. I know I'm supposed to be grounded for a while. But I've been wondering…how long is a while?"

Tanner suggested, "How 'bout you talk this over with your mom and dad during your phone call tomorrow night?"

"All right," said DeDe. "I think I will."

That day, Wednesday—and Thursday, too—Crystal finished whipping the office into presentable shape. She ran up two sets of simple curtains on Kelly's sewing machine and covered the throw pillows she'd bought. The contrasting fabrics were all shades of blue and green that looked great with the brown and perked up the place considerably.

Thursday night, when DeDe called her parents, she asked about the sleepover. It was agreed that as long as she continued behaving so well, she could go to the party Saturday night.

Friday, Tanner brought in a brawny-looking buddy, and the two of them moved the tall file cabinets into the front office. Crystal spent the rest of the day working with the Excel spreadsheets Tanner used to keep track of his accounts. She set up a form for his appointment schedule and got him to spend a few hours going over his calendar with her so she could transfer the data to the computer.

That evening she told him that on Monday the office would be officially open for business.

* * *

Tanner was off to work at seven Saturday morning. He was trying to track down some grifter who'd absconded with the savings of several gullible senior citizens. He said he hoped to be home by late afternoon.

DeDe had a dance lesson at nine. After the lesson, she came home and went without protest to her room, where she did her homework—calling Crystal in twice to ask advice on the book report she was writing. They broke for grilled cheese sandwiches at noon.

At three, Crystal drove her over to Devon Marie's.

"I'll miss my call tonight with Mom and Dad," DeDe reported solemnly as Crystal eased her car in at the curb in front of the Spanish-style two-story house. "But it's okay. Dad said I could call them tomorrow night instead."

"You can tell them all about the party then."

DeDe beamed. "That's right." She leaned across the console and gave Crystal a big kiss. "Thanks, Crystal."

"Any time."

Crystal popped the trunk and DeDe got out her sleeping bag and bulging backpack. She ran up the front walk and paused to wave when Devon Marie opened the door. Crystal hit the horn once in response and put the car in gear.

Since she had some free time, she stopped at the office and worked on the filing system for an hour and a half. Tanner called while she was there.

"I'll be a little later than I thought. Maybe seven? A couple of leads panned out and I want to follow through on them."

She promised to hold dinner for him and went over to her apartment to pick up her mail and water the plants. Doris saw she was in and dropped by. They sat at the table and drank iced tea. Crystal asked after Nigel.

"Ornery as ever," said her neighbor. "But at least he hasn't disappeared since the last time you helped me search for him. And how's that young man of yours?"

Crystal felt wonder then. And a fierce sort of joy. Tanner *was* her young man. And she was proud to claim him. She'd come a long way in a week and a day.

She let out a happy sigh. "Oh, Doris. I can't tell you. He's the best and then some."

Doris shook a wrinkled brown finger. "Snap him up. Don't hesitate. These days the good ones are few and far between."

Crystal stopped at the supermarket and filled a cart with groceries. She visited the meat counter and chose a couple of fat New York steaks for that night. Tanner loved red meat. She didn't, or she hadn't until the past couple of months.

Lately, she craved beef and a lot of it, rare. So strange. It had been the same for her the other time, with the baby they took away from her. She'd eaten beef and more beef and loved every bite.

Her lost baby...

Crystal stared into the middle distance, sending up a prayer—that her daughter was safe and well and loved. And happy. Always, she prayed that her lost little girl was happy.

For years, after she left the dark, quiet house of her childhood and struck out on her own, she'd tried to forget about the little girl they'd taken away from her. She'd told herself that surely the baby had gone to a good home. Surely she was doing well, with two parents who loved her and took tender care of her.

Surely the best and wisest course was to try to forget, to move on. Let it go.

But lately, since she'd been drawn back to Northern California, and especially since she found there would be a second child, her thoughts of the first one were becoming more frequent, her prayers more fervent. Crystal was beginning to admit to herself that she needed information. She needed, finally, to know that her first child truly was safe and happy.

She had to go to her parents, ask them again to tell her where her baby had gone. Yes, they'd always absolutely refused to tell her, no matter how much she pleaded with them, but maybe now, after all these years, they would see things differently.

Soon, she was thinking. I'll go face them, talk to them, *beg* them all over again to help me find her.

"Here you go, now." The white-aproned man behind the meat counter held out the wrapped steaks.

Crystal blinked. "Oh! Thank you." She took the package and put it in the cart and rolled away down the bread aisle.

She needed to tell Tanner about the child she'd lost. Tanner might even be able to help her find out where the little girl was now.

Yes. She needed to tell him.

And she would.

Soon.

Tanner pulled up in front of Kelly's house at 6:58 p.m. Right on time.

He'd spent the morning and most of the afternoon

tracking the SOB who had stolen money from senior citizens. When he'd done what he could on that front, he'd gone back to his house and booted up his computer.

He was building a file on Crystal's lost child. He made some progress on the Internet, accessing a number of sites only available for a hefty fee. He hadn't learned a lot, but it was often a slow process with something like this. He'd gotten a few steps along the road to the truth today.

Probably, they were steps he shouldn't even be taking. But he had this idea that now that he'd come this far, he should go all the way—find that little girl and have the information ready. In case Crystal wanted to know. It would be his gift to her, a chance to answer the hardest question.

Would she want the answer?

He had no idea, though he did have a kind of bad feeling, deep down about this. Not about the little girl so much—he wasn't far along enough in the hunt for her to get any kind of feeling about her yet. His bad feeling was about Crystal, that she wasn't going to like it much when she found out he'd gone behind her back to learn more about the secret she'd yet to share with him.

If she'd wanted him to do anything about finding her daughter, she would have told him so. But so far, she hadn't even managed to tell him that there'd *been* a daughter in the first place. So he had a pretty good sense that when the truth came out, he was going to be in some serious hot water with her.

But it was his nature, to get the answers—especially in a situation like this, where his gut told him that Crys needed this, needed to know what had happened to her child. It was his nature to dig beneath the surface, and bring up whatever might be hiding down there.

His nature. And his curse.

Inside the house, he called her name.

No answer. He went through the empty rooms, looking for her. In the kitchen, he found the oven on. He turned on the light in there and saw a fat pair of foil-wrapped potatoes. He opened the fridge: two big steaks on a platter.

She was here somewhere. He spotted her purse, looped with bright chains and hardware hearts, on the china cabinet, next to the phone.

He went to the slider that opened onto the backyard—and saw her through the glass. She lay on a chaise beneath the branches of a maple tree, wearing a shirt the color of a ripe peach and yellow shorts.

A book lay open across her stomach. She seemed to be napping, looking so peaceful. So beautiful and sweet.

Taking care to do it silently, Tanner pushed open the door.

Crystal heard Cisco whining and the soft slap of his tail on the concrete. But she was riding the edge of slumber, so she tuned out the sounds and faded back toward sleep.

Then she felt a warm breath across her cheek. And tender lips brushing hers.

She opened her eyes and said his name on a happy sigh. "Tanner…" She scooted over a little to make room for him, and he sat beside her on the chaise.

"I should have let you sleep," he said.

She reached up a hand and hooked it around the back of his neck, urging him down to her. "Kiss me some more."

So he kissed her, lots of kisses—on her lips, her cheeks, down the length of her throat to that place where her collarbones meet. He kissed the spot where her pulse beat, quickening, making her blood flow hot and eager.

For him. For his touch, his kiss, the feel of his body pressing down on hers. She wanted him. All of him.

He unbuttoned her shirt and kissed the slopes of her breasts, easing her bra out of the way, revealing nipples already hard with wanting him.

Needing him.

When he slipped one arm beneath her shoulders and one under her knees and lifted her high, she didn't object.

"We're alone tonight," he whispered.

"Oh, yes. I know." She pressed her mouth to the side of his neck, loving the taste of him, the delicious feel of his skin against her lips.

"If you're going to tell me no, you'd better do it now."

She pressed her teeth to the spot she'd just kissed and sucked, not hard enough to make a mark. But almost.

He let out a moan. "That felt like a yes to me."

"Oh, Tanner. It was. A definite yes...."

Chapter Twelve

Tanner carried her through the house and into the guest room, swinging the door shut with his foot, leaving Cisco on the other side.

"Poor Cisco," she whispered, pressing her forehead to his, thinking how she'd wanted him the first night she had met him—of their crazy, wild secret affair that was always supposed to be finished and yet somehow never was. Thinking that, though it hardly seemed possible to want him more than she had at first, she did. She wanted him more now. More every day. Every hour. Every minute.

Her body ached with the need for him.

"Cisco will live," he whispered. So gently, he lowered her to the big bed. "Later, I'll give him some of my steak."

She brushed the thick, silky hair at his temple. "How did you know there was steak?"

"I know everything. I'm a private investigator. And right now, I'm in the mood to investigate every inch of you."

"Oh, well. That's good. I really need investigating."

"I know you do. Kiss me."

She obeyed, offering her mouth to him. He took it, his tongue sliding in, sweeping the inner surfaces, making her moan deep in her throat and lift up her body to him, at the same time as she tried to pull him down to her.

But he wouldn't go. He took her wrists and gently placed them on the pillow, to either side of her head.

And then he broke the wet, hot kiss just enough to whisper against her lips, "Don't move." That made her moan some more. He put a finger to her mouth—and she sucked it right inside. "You drive me crazy," he said on a groan, as she wrapped her tongue around his finger. He slid it free a moment later, to kiss her lips some more.

As his mouth played on hers, he finished unbuttoning her shirt. He smoothed it wide, then traced the lacy cups of her bra, up the swell of one breast, down to the center of her chest, up to the crest again.

Her bra hooked in front, so he undid it and peeled the cups wide, murmuring compliments and hot encouragements. She fisted her hands on the pillows to keep from reaching, from spearing her fingers into his hair as he kissed her breast, drawing the nipple into his hot mouth, sucking until she cried out with the pleasure of it.

His hand strayed downward. She lifted her hips toward his touch, so eager, so hungry. For him. Always.

For him…

He undid the button at the top of her shorts and took the zipper down in a smooth, even glide. His fingers eased their way in, beneath the silk of her panties and lower. He cupped her mound, pressing.

She cried out again. "Oh, yes. There. Please…"

And then he parted her, knowing fingers slipping in, finding her wet and so ready for him. He knew right where to touch, to stroke, to pet.

She tried to reach for him. But tenderly, with his free arm, he guided her hands back onto the pillow again.

And he went on stroking her, making love to her with those magic fingers of his. He lowered his mouth to hers and he kissed her, so deeply, so thoroughly.

She moaned into his mouth as her body bloomed for him, as ripples of heat and sensation spiked high and spread out in hot, lovely ripples from the feminine heart of her to the tips of her toes, the crown of her head, the pads of her fingers.

"Oh, Tanner. Oh, yes…" She said his name over again. And again. And again.

And then she lay limp, pleasured. Content.

But he was by no means finished with her. "Now I want you naked…." He kissed her lips and the tip of her chin.

"You can have me naked," she whispered. It wasn't the least bit difficult to get there. Everything was either unbuttoned, unsnapped or unzipped. Sitting up, she eased out of her shirt and tossed her bra away. She shimmied her shorts and panties down and off. She grinned. "Your turn. In fact, I'll be glad to help." She reached for him.

He caught her shoulders and guided her back down. "Uh-uh. You stay right there. This won't take a minute."

And it didn't. He stripped off his shirt and threw it

to the floor, pulled off his boots and got rid of his socks. Then he stood, pulled his button fly wide and shoved down his jeans and boxers in one move.

He stepped out of them and kicked them aside. She laced her fingers under her head and admired the view. He had those broad shoulders that went on for days. And a hard, strong chest she loved to lean on. He had washboard abs and, jutting out from a nest of black hair, the hard proof that he wanted her every bit as much as she wanted him.

She said, "You are so beautiful. The most beautiful man in the world…"

He smiled. Slowly. "Not one-half as beautiful as you." He sat on the side of the bed. "You're like some fairy princess, Crys. You know that? Even DeDe says so. All this amazing gold hair." He caught a handful of it, wrapped it around his fist, slowly let it slide free. "And your face, like an angel."

"Tanner." She lowered her lashes and gave him her most demure little smile.

He frowned. "What?"

"I'm no angel…."

He bent close. "Well, and that's the best part, now isn't it?"

She lifted her hands from the pillows then. And he didn't try to stop her. She pulled his mouth down hard on hers and kissed him, taking the lead, slipping her tongue beyond his lips and tasting him deeply as her hungry hands caressed his hard shoulders, the silky, muscular sweep of his chest and lower, down over his flat, hard-ridged belly.

He gasped when she encircled him. And then he moaned as she began to stroke him. She knew just how he liked it—not too fast, not too slow, long and tight and smooth.

The kiss they shared was endless and wet and deep and perfect as she continued to pleasure him, using the slick moisture that wept from the tip, rubbing it over him, making it easier to get that steady, arousing glide he liked the most.

He warned against her lips, "I can't…last…"

And she whispered, "I know. It's good. I want you to come for me…."

And then he groaned as he went over. She stroked him, milking him, pressing him finally against her bare belly, feeling the lovely, slick wetness spurt onto her skin, loving the hard, insistent pulsing of him within her encircling grip.

When he was done, she scooted over to make room for him. He flopped down beside her, spent in the truest sense of the word.

She stared at the ceiling, grinning.

He growled low in his throat. "Pleased with yourself, are you?"

And she laughed. "You know what they say: What's good for the goose…"

"Yeah, right. But now I'm going to need time to recover."

"No problem. I can wait. You know, build the anticipation. That's always fun."

He rolled off the edge of the bed and onto his feet.

She reached for him. "Don't go."

"Be right back." And he was, with a damp, warm towel. He wiped her stomach clean. And then he sat beside her again and rested his hand there. "Still flat."

"Not for long." She pressed her hand over his.

"I can't wait to see you all round and ripe with my baby."

She looked into those fine, dark eyes and the words were right there, filling her heart, on the tip of her tongue. *I love you, Tanner. So very much…*

She held them back. It all felt too fragile right then. Too new. And there was the past, the hardest secret, the one she had yet to share with him. About the baby. About her parents and the choice they'd taken away from her.

About the cruel boy who had hurt her so bad.

Somehow, it seemed important—that he know everything, that she have no secrets from him when the time came to tell him how he had managed to lay claim to her heart.

Uh-uh. Tonight was for pleasure—shared, freely given. Pleasure for the first time without denials.

He was watching her face. "What?"

"Just thinking…"

"Tell me."

"Well, do you realize tonight will be the first time we've ever made love without telling each other how it's going to be the *last* time? I call that progress."

He grunted. "If you say so."

"I do. And how about dinner—you know, in the meantime? The potatoes should be ready by now."

He bent close and kissed her. Then he knelt to grab his boxers and jeans. "Get dressed. I'll start the grill."

Tanner cooked the steaks. It didn't take long.

He brought them in on a platter and Crystal had the table set and the salad and potatoes all ready. She gave him one of those smiles, and he realized that he was already fully recovered from what she'd done to him a half an hour before.

He wanted to sweep her up into his arms and carry her off down the hall again.

But the dinner did look damn good. So they ate, sharing more than a few tasty bits with Cisco, who wolfed down what they tossed him and then curled up in the corner for a nice after-dinner snooze.

When they were finished, she picked up her plate and reached for his. He caught her wrist.

"Tanner…" Her voice reproached him. But her eyes invited.

He pulled her into his lap. She felt excellent there— immediately rocking a little, just to drive him wild.

He cupped her breast and smoothed her golden curls out of his way and then kissed her neck until she gave in with a sigh and set her plate down on top of his.

"Better," he muttered, catching her chin with a finger, guiding her face around to his.

Her lips tempted him. He surrendered, pulling her close, claiming a long, sweet kiss.

Already, he was hard for her. Hungry. Needing.

It had been way too long since he'd been inside her— two weeks, since, by his calculations, the second time she tried to tell him about the baby, and failed.

He smiled at the thought of that.

"What?" she demanded.

"Nothing. Everything. Kiss me."

She gave him her mouth again. He took it, spearing his tongue in, breathing deeply through his nose, sucking in the scent of her, licking up the taste.…

No woman, ever in his lifetime, had had her scent or her special, sweet flavor. How could a woman seem so wrong from the first—and yet turn out to be exactly, amazingly right?

As he kissed her, he smoothed a hand down her sleek thigh. She laughed against his lips and took his signal, sliding off his lap just enough that she could turn and sit facing him, one leg on either side of him.

She was too tempting that way. He cupped her fully, over her yellow shorts. He traced the side of his thumb along the tender opening that was shielded from him by her clothes.

She moaned at that and pushed her hips against him. He traced the shape of her again, feeling the slight dampness through the fabric that spoke of her need— as powerful as his.

He wanted her naked, right now, here in his lap. He set about removing the clothes he'd gotten off her once before. He unbuttoned her shirt and pushed it over her smooth shoulders and down her arms until it dropped free.

He unhooked her bra, which was the same flaming pink as her panties. Easing it over her shoulders and down her arms, he dropped it to the floor.

Her breasts were so beautiful, full and ripe and sweet, begging for his tongue. He took them—one and then other, sucking the nipples into his mouth, teasing them with his teeth, until she tossed her head back and cried out his name and her hair swung like warm silk against the backs of his hands.

He needed those shorts off her, needed those pretty panties out of his way....

She seemed to know that—or maybe it was only that

she needed the same thing. Rocking her weight onto her feet, she stepped clear of him long enough to shove down her shorts and get rid of the panties.

He wasn't idle. He pulled open the buttons on his jeans and eased himself free of his boxers.

And then she came back to him. Lowering herself by slow, sweet, unbearable degrees, she took him within her. The sensation was like no other, to be surrounded fully by her hot, slick heat.

He fisted his hands in her swinging mane of hair and buried his face in the curve her neck. She stretched her throat back for him, giving him free access to the satiny skin there. He kissed her and scraped his teeth along that smooth flesh—but not too hard. And then he licked where his teeth had been.

A low moan escaped her. He lifted his hips to her, giving her more. And she took him. So deep. So completely. So exactly what he hungered for.

The world spun away from him. There was only her heat and her wetness around him, only the glorious curtain of her hair, the roundness of her breasts against him, the sweetness of her lips pressed to his, the beautiful sounds of her moans and soft cries.

He lifted into her and retreated. She met each needful stroke, until there was nothing but pleasure, shared and expanding. They moved together, in a rhythm so right that his body was her body, her pleasure was his....

She made a low, sighing sound, a sound like a purr or a feminine growl, as she rose to the finish. He was so completely hers by then that he could do nothing else but follow her upward, surging high into her as her climax exploded and her inner muscles worked him, tightening, releasing—only to tighten again.

And again.

He let her take him. Up high and still higher. His climax rushed over him, ripping through the center of him, turning him inside out. He surged up into her.

She held him close and tight and steady as the finish rolled through him. A final shudder racked him. She pressed her lips to his throat and softly whispered his name.

Chapter Thirteen

They went to bed together that night in the guest room, making love before sleep took them—and then waking hours before dawn to make love again.

When daylight came, Tanner woke first. It took him a second or two to realize where he was: in bed with Crystal.

She had her warm, soft foot tucked behind his knee, and her hand rested on his shoulder. He listened for the rhythm of her breathing, shallow and even. Still asleep.

He lay very still, kind of drinking in the moment. A whole night with Crystal. It didn't get much better than that.

Moving slowly, trying not to disturb her, he turned over so he could see her. She looked so innocent in sleep, her hair tangled on the pillow behind her, curls spreading everywhere—over the blankets, across her cheek.

As he watched, she sighed and muttered something in her sleep.

And then, slowly, she came awake. She pushed back the covers, smoothed those tangled curls away from her face. He watched her eyes open.

She blinked and yawned. "You're staring at me."

"Yes, I am."

Her eyelids drifted shut again. She sighed once more, a contented sort of sound. He thought she might sleep again.

But no. She asked, with her eyes still closed. "What time is it?"

He could see the bedside clock. "Eight forty-five."

"Um," she said. And then she was looking at him. She wrapped her arms around the pillow, snuggled into it and gave him a frown. "What?"

He smoothed her hair, caressed her cheek. He traced the delicate curve of her ear. "What do you mean, what?"

She caught his wrist, pressing her lips to the pad of flesh on the inside of his hand, below his thumb. "You've got that look—the one that says you're trying to figure out how to say something."

He went for it. "When Kelly and Mitch get back, I want you to come and live with me."

She stared. And then she rolled over and pushed back the covers. She sent him an over-the-shoulder glance. "Just a minute." She jumped to her feet and started walking. He admired the view of her fine bare backside until she disappeared into the bathroom.

He heard the toilet flush and water running and then she appeared again. Still naked. She hadn't covered herself in a robe or anything. He took that as a good sign.

Plus, she was every bit as gorgeous from the front as from the rear. His body reacted—he ordered it to chill. There were, he reminded himself, more important things than sex, though when he was looking at Crystal naked, it was a real chore to remember what those things were.

He lifted the covers, inviting her back in the bed with him. With no hesitation, she came to him, sliding in beside him. He tucked the blankets around her.

She whispered, "Live with you…"

He wanted to ask for more. For everything. Forever. But he figured a step at a time was the way to go with her. "Yeah. Live in my house, sleep in my bed. See how it works out, the two of us, together. I think we owe that to our baby—I mean, given that things have been working out pretty well up till now."

She sat up suddenly. "I have a better idea."

He watched her, feeling wary. "What idea?"

"You can come live with me."

It wasn't what he'd had in mind. "Uh…"

She pinched up her pretty nose. "I know that look. You don't want to sleep on my futon." She had two of them—the one in the living room, the couch. And one in the bedroom.

"I like my house," he argued. "It's comfortable."

"It's as brown as your office was before I added some color."

"So. You can add color. You can do whatever you want to it. Just come and live in it."

"For how long?"

Forever, he thought. But he spoke with more care. "We'll make it open-ended. You can keep your own place. I'll pay the rent for you, if that helps."

She wrapped the blankets closer around herself and huffed out a breath. "Of course you won't pay my rent. I have a job, remember? Thanks to you."

He pried her hand free of its grip on the blanket and held it between both of his. "Think about it. Last night was our first whole night in the same bed."

She eased her hand free and slanted him a look. "So you think we need more of that?"

"More sex with you more often? Damn straight. I always need that—and not only sex. We need more of waking up in the morning together, more of working together and living together."

She reached up then and brushed the hair at his temple. "Oh, Tanner…"

His heart did something scary inside his chest. He was certain then. It was *the* moment. She would tell him her deepest secret at last, speak to him of the child she'd lost. "Yeah?"

But then she looked away, shook her head.

He tried a little nudge. "Whatever it is, you can tell me. I can take it. You know I can."

She still wouldn't face him. "I know you can take it." A small, sad laugh escaped her. "But can I?"

"Crys…" He dared to reach for her, to brush her cheek with the side of his hand. "Come on."

And at last, she turned to him. He saw in her eyes that the moment had passed. She wasn't going to tell him. Not now.

But then she said, "Living with you, huh? At your place…"

"Yeah," he answered. "Live with me. Please."

She offered him her hand again. He took it. They shook.

And then he pulled her into his arms and kissed her good and hard to seal the deal.

The next week went by without a hitch. DeDe was almost her old self again—only a little more serious. A little more grown-up. She spent an hour every other night on the phone with her parents, reporting all the details of her life at home. She followed the calendar on the fridge without argument, getting her chores and her homework done on time.

Crystal spent Monday through Friday, nine to three, at Dark Horse Investigations. She handled Tanner's daytime calls and scheduled appointments for him. She set up a payables and receivables procedure, writing the checks and leaving them, with their accompanying paperwork, on his desk for his signature. Though he was accustomed to meeting with clients anywhere but at the office, he actually started coming in a couple of times a day and counseling with clients there. And three times that week, she got new clients for him because she was there when they walked through the office door.

Thursday afternoon before she left for Kelly's house, Tanner told her she was invaluable.

She laughed. "See, there's a benefit to working so many different jobs. I have wide range of experience to offer. There's just about no department in any given office that I can't figure out how to run."

"Like I said, invaluable." He held out his hand to her.

Because they were alone in the office right then, she rose and went into his waiting arms.

Friday night, DeDe had a sleepover at Mia Lu's. Which meant Tanner spent the night in the guest room with Crystal.

She was the one who woke first Saturday morning. She watched his face as he slept beside her and thought how every day she grew to love him a little more. She wondered sometimes now how she'd lived her life without him in it.

They worked together.

And now they would live together. *Really* live together—share the same bed, wake up every morning side-by-side.

Soon she really did need to tell him all the things that were so hard to say. And she would. Truly.

Soon.

At four-thirty that afternoon, Kelly and Mitch got home. They both looked tan and happy. And more relaxed than Crystal had ever seen either of them.

After hugs all around, Tanner and Crystal, who'd already packed their cars, said goodbye. Kelly insisted they both show up the next day for the traditional family Sunday dinner.

"We'll be here," Tanner promised, and realized too late that he'd spoken for Crystal. Mitch and Kelly shared a look—and Tanner backpedaled. "I mean, I'll be here. And you'll come too, won't you, Crystal?"

She had to fight the urge to chuckle. "Tomorrow, then," she said. "Around five, right?" And they got the heck out of there before questions could be asked.

They drove off in their separate cars, just like old times. She got all the way to her place before she spotted

Tanner in her rearview mirror. He eased the Mustang into the space beside her Camaro, and they met on the walkway between the two cars.

He teased, "You didn't think you could escape me, did you?"

"As if I would want to." She grabbed his hand. "Come on in. I want to get a few more things."

"Just as long as you're coming home with me tonight…"

"You know that I am."

In the apartment, she went to the bedroom and began pulling clothing from the drawers and closet and folding it all on the bed.

He leaned in the doorway. "You see that look Mitch and Kelly gave each other?"

"You mean when you put your foot in it?"

He glanced down at his boots. "We do have to tell them."

She dropped the stack of shirts she was carrying onto the bed and went to him, resting her hands on his broad chest and feeling the steady beat of his heart beneath her palms. "I know. But it didn't seem right to do it today— I mean, with them just getting off the plane and all."

"Tomorrow night at dinner, then?"

She winced. "I was thinking of a more…private approach. I could have lunch with Kelly—say, Monday? And I'll tell her then."

"So what you're saying is, I get Mitch."

"Why not? It will…be a bonding moment for the two of you."

He shook his head. "Mitch and me. Bonding. Now I'm getting really scared."

She touched the side of his face. It was deliciously rough with five o'clock shadow. "I know you guys have had issues…"

"*Issues* is putting it mildly. He resented the hell out of me. And when he disappeared, leaving Kelly pregnant, I was not his biggest fan. Kelly asked me to look for him. I did, but not as hard as I could have."

"But now he's found. Things are…good between you, right?"

"Yeah. They're okay. We're past all the garbage. We're movin' on."

"So it would be…a good approach, I think. I tell Kelly. You tell Mitch."

"He's pretty protective of you, you know? What if he goes all big brother on my ass?"

"Are you kidding? He's going to be glad—you'll see."

He guided a loose curl behind her ear. "I know that look in your eye. This isn't a choice, is it?"

"You can do it. It will be fine."

Crystal followed Tanner to his house. When they got there, he helped carry her stuff in. There was plenty of room in his walk-in closet for anything she wanted to put in there. And there was a dresser without much in it. He emptied it and said it was hers.

"Hungry?" he asked when everything was put away.

"Starving." She didn't mean for food.

He looked into her eyes and slowly smiled.

Later, they got dressed and went out to a little café he knew of nearby. Then they went grocery shopping.

He never kept a lot in the fridge, anyway, but since the week at Kelly's, his pantry was definitely bare.

They went to bed early, telling each other they would go right to sleep. But it was all too new and exciting—to settle into bed together and know that neither of them would be getting up and leaving later. Their lovemaking was sweet and slow. They lay on their sides, facing each other and moved together in a rhythm like waves. She thought again of her love for him.

But she didn't tell him. Yet. She knew the right time was coming, though.

Soon.

Tanner had to work in the morning, so Crystal went over to her place to get some pots and pans and her favorite paring knife. She stopped in at Doris's. The older woman gave her tea, and Crystal explained she'd be staying at Tanner's for a while.

Doris said, "I know you two are going to be blissfully happy."

Crystal beamed. "I like your attitude, Doris. I truly do."

At Tanner's, she put the pots and pans away in his cabinets and looked around at the tan walls and brown leather furniture. Ugh. At least the bed was big and comfy. In a few days, she'd get down to figuring out inexpensive ways to brighten the house up a little. And she would move the furniture around to make it more inviting. The place called out for some serious feng shui.

But at the moment, she needed a nap.

The backyard wasn't bad. There were trees. And a nice square of patio, decked out with padded lawn furniture. She chose a comfy chair and a plastic ottoman, and she snoozed until Tanner got back at four-thirty.

It was just too ridiculous to drive over to Kelly's in separate cars, so they went together. On the way, they agreed that if anyone asked, they'd tell the simple truth. As in, *Yes, we drove over here together.* Period. End of explanation.

No one asked. Crystal thought she saw a couple of strange glances dart between Kelly and Mitch. But that was it.

After they cleared off the meal, they all played Wii bowling. It did Crystal's heart good to hear DeDe's happy laughter. The kid really did seem to be getting past her anger at her father and the changes he was making in her life.

Before Crystal and Tanner left, Kelly drew her aside. "Lunch," she said. "Tomorrow. Don't try to get out of it. You *know* we need to talk."

Crystal hugged her. "I think you must have read my mind."

They agreed on the restaurant and the time.

In the car, Tanner said, "Mitch asked me to meet him for lunch."

"You mean, before *you* had a chance to ask *him*?"

"That's right."

"You think, maybe, they're onto us?"

"Looks pretty damn likely to me."

"We knew it," said Kelly when Crystal told her that she and Tanner had decided to move in together.

"I was thinking that maybe you did."

"I can't believe I didn't pick up on it before Saturday."

"Kell," Crystal reminded her gently. "You've had a

lot to deal with in your own life lately. You haven't had much spare energy for worrying about what your brother and your best friend are up to."

"How long has this been going on?"

"Oh, since about the first time he and I saw each other."

"Oh. My. Gosh."

"Put your iced tea down. I don't want you to spit when you hear the rest."

Eyes wide, Kelly pushed her glass away. "There's more?"

"I quit my job with Bandley and Schinker—and Tanner hired me to run his office for him."

"You're kidding."

"Uh-uh. And I'm pregnant."

Kelly threw back her head and let out a screech. The people at the tables nearby turned to stare. She put her hand over her mouth. "Oops. Sorry…" she said to the restaurant in general. Then she leaned across the table and whispered to Crystal. "How far along?"

"A couple of months."

"I know my brother. He wants to get married, doesn't he?"

"Yeah. I think he does."

Kelly slapped the tabletop in disbelief. "You *think?* He hasn't asked you?"

"Oh, Kell. I haven't given him a chance. At first, I insisted I wouldn't marry him. He was so sweet and understanding about it. But then he immediately came up with this plan how we should be together to watch DeDe, how he would take the daybed in your office and we could see how it went, living in the same house— and then he offered me a job. And when you guys came back from your honeymoon, he talked me into moving in with him…."

"Only one thing really matters. You love him, right?"

"Oh, Kell…"

"You do. It's written all over your face. And he loves you. He wouldn't be moving you in with him if he didn't, wouldn't be looking at you the way he did Sunday night. I know you want to marry him. Let him ask you."

"I will. Soon…"

"She lives with you, she works for you and she's pregnant with your baby," said Mitch. "Marry her."

Tanner wasn't arguing. "I will. As soon as I can get her to say yes."

"You've asked her, then?"

Tanner didn't answer. He ate a bite of his steak sandwich.

"What the hell?" said Mitch. "You *haven't* asked her."

Tanner dropped the remains of the sandwich back on the plate and grabbed his napkin. "It's not like she gave me a chance. She told me she was having my baby, and in the next breath she told me she would never marry me. I've been workin' every angle since then to get her to see that we'd be good together. I think I'm making progress."

Mitch was not impressed with his excuses. "So pop the damn question."

"I'm getting there. But you know her. She's all heart and light and sweetness. On the surface. But she's got some big damn secrets, Mitch. Things she holds inside herself, things she won't tell me about so I can maybe help her with them. I can't get through to those secrets."

Mitch shrugged. "Yeah. So?"

"You know what I'm talking about, right?"

Mitch glanced away.

Tanner put the pressure on. "Right?"

And Mitch met his eyes. "I'll say this. I've been a paranoid SOB a lot of my life. When I met Crystal, we went out a few times. It was pretty clear from the first that it wasn't going to be a sex thing between us. That made me suspicious. That I liked her without knowing a damn thing about her—I liked her and I didn't even want to get in bed with her."

Tanner couldn't imagine any man not wanting to get in bed with Crystal. But the fact that Mitch didn't want to and never had was fine with him.

Mitch went on. "Then she comes to me and tells me she's had a numinous experience. *Numinous?* I had to go look up the word. She's realized, she says, that I'm her brother—no, not by blood, but in the ways that *really* matter. About then, I knew that even though I liked her and wanted to trust her, I had to find out what was up with her. I hired a detective. He took a couple of weeks and worked up a file on her. But by then, I was realizing I didn't care what was going on with her. She'd told me that she'd remade her life, that she'd changed her name and started over. I believed her. And I decided, for once in my life, I was going to just go with my gut on a personal level the way I do when it comes to business. I paid off the detective and threw the file he gave me in the trash."

Tanner wanted clarification. "You're saying you never read it?"

"That's right. I never read it. I didn't need to read it. She's the best damn friend a man could have. She's a straight-ahead, honest person when it comes to how she's always dealt with me. And her secrets are her business. Her private business. And if the day comes she ever wants to tell me about them, I'm here for her. You hear what I'm saying?"

Tanner did hear it. "Loud and clear."

"Let her tell you her secrets in her own way, when and if she's ready. For now, tell her you love her. Ask her to marry you. Forget the rest of it."

It was good advice. Too bad Tanner already knew the secret she couldn't bring herself to share with him.

Chapter Fourteen

The week passed. May faded into June. Another week went by. The days got hotter and the nights more sultry.

Tanner was a happy man. Crystal constantly amazed him.

She was a damn fine assistant. The best. How could the woman he'd always thought of as a flake be so organized?

His business worked so much more smoothly, in just the few weeks she'd been handling appointments, dispatching his daytime calls, keeping his files updated for him and making sure he didn't blow off any of the bills. His repeat clients were nuts about her. They told him how she "took care" of them. She had that special talent for handling the edgy types, and for diffusing the occasional tense situation.

At home, she moved the furniture around and added

throw pillows, curtains and bright pictures here and there. She brought in greenery. He gave her a bad time about it—said if he'd wanted to live in a jungle, he'd have moved to the Amazon.

But the truth was, he liked it, liked how much more comfortable the house was, how relaxing it was to live in. Crystal had made it that way.

Sometimes at night, after making sweet love with her, he'd lie there and listen to her breathing even out as she drifted off to sleep. He'd wonder how he had gotten along without her. He'd think of his brother-in-law's advice and know that Mitch was right.

Tanner didn't care anymore about the past she wouldn't share with him. He'd found out more than he should have, more than he had any right to learn without her permission. He couldn't unlearn what he knew. The truth would remain, locked in the bottom drawer of his desk in his office at home. Until the day she decided she was ready to deal with it.

If she ever did.

But for him, what mattered was their life together, the sight of her in the morning, across the breakfast table, her face scrubbed clean of makeup, grinning as she ate another slice of bacon. What mattered was the two of them wrapped up in bed, whispering together, sharing kisses. Making love.

What mattered was their life together and the home they would make for their coming child. He had her in his house, at his office and in his bed, too, at last. More than his next breath, he wanted her to stay with him.

It was time to take Mitch's advice.

On the second Tuesday in June, when she thought he

was working, he went to a jewelry store on K Street and bought her a ring. Then he called her at the office.

"Dark Horse Investigations. This is Crystal."

"Take off a little early. Go home and put on your prettiest dress."

She laughed. "Who *is* this?"

"The man who's got six-thirty reservations at the best steak house in town."

"All right. Now, you've got my attention."

"I figured a sentence with the word *steak* in it would do it."

She faked a big sigh. "Sadly, though, I can no longer zip up my prettiest dress." She was getting rounder. He thought the extra weight looked good on her. Really good.

"It doesn't matter what you wear. You're beautiful. The most beautiful woman I've ever known."

"Tanner." Her voice was soft as a kiss, suddenly.

"Yeah?"

"What a lovely thing to say."

"I don't know about lovely. But I know it's the truth."

At the restaurant, they got a booth in a private alcove. They took their time ordering. And when they did, they had it all. Appetizer, salad and main course; then they shared one of those chocolate volcano things that when you cut it open oozed more chocolate.

When they were finished, she put her hand on her round stomach and said, "That does it. After tonight, I'm not going to be fitting into my *second* prettiest dress."

"Fine with me. I like you naked anyway." He had the ring in his pocket and had planned to propose over dessert.

But now he was thinking it would be better at home. Where it was truly private, with just the two of them.

Crystal knew what was coming. She could see it in his dark eyes.

He was the handsomest man alive in his white dress shirt and black slacks. And she had never been happier.

Too bad she was also scared to death.

She knew what she had to do before she could say yes. She needed to tell him her last secret. The hardest one of all.

"You're quiet," he said on the way back to the house, sending her a questioning glance before focusing again on the road before them.

"Just thinking."

Talk about an understatement. Her mind raced. Why, she wondered, should this be so hard? Why did she hold it within so tightly? Why, when she knew she could trust the man beside her, had she still been unable to share the toughest truth with him?

As she asked herself the questions, her heart knew the answers. Within her, at the very center of her, there was an empty space, a space of hurt and sadness, of not knowing. In order to survive, she had moved on, made a new life, learned to let go.

But within, the emptiness, the pain and the questions lingered.

For weeks, she had known this night was coming. Now it was upon her. She was so happy.

And so terrified.

He reached across, caught her hand, brought it to his lips. She sent him a tender smile.

They were at the house in no time. The garage door rumbled up and he pulled his car in next to hers. The door went down behind them as he turned off the engine.

In the sudden quiet, he shifted his body in the driver's seat. His eyes gleamed in the dim light.

Love, she thought. I love this man. And she knew gratitude. She'd made a full, rich life for herself in the years since she'd left her parents' house behind. An independent life. She'd been content, on her own, without a special man to love. She'd been complete.

But now, somehow, with Tanner—and with the new baby that was coming—she felt *more* than complete, somehow. She felt blessed. Fulfilled.

He leaned close and she met him halfway. His kiss, as always, curled her toes and set a bunch of butterflies loose in her midsection.

When he pulled away, he kissed the tip of her nose. "Let's go in." He grabbed his sport coat from the backseat.

They went in through the utility room and on to the kitchen. A long tiled counter separated it from the living room, with breakfast nook and dining room branching off at either end.

It looked good, she thought. Inviting and attractive. The changes she'd made—rearranging the furniture, adding more color—had helped a lot to make the house more comfortable.

Home, she thought. This is my home now.

All she had to do was get the words out, tell him the final truth. And they would have it all—everything that mattered: love and family. And forever.

Tanner hung back by the jut of the kitchen counter, his sport coat over his arm. She glanced his way and saw nervousness in the quirk of his mouth, in the slight frown that had formed between his dark brows.

Tenderness flooded through her. She gave him a wide smile and held out her hand to him.

"You want some of that tea of yours, or something?" he asked.

"Uh-uh. No tea. Not now." She waited for him, her hand outstretched—in the center of the room.

He approached her. Dropping the coat over the back of a chair, he took the hand she offered. She lifted her mouth to him.

After an achingly sweet brush of a kiss, he whispered, "I love you, Crys. I thought we were all wrong for each other, but we turned out somehow to be so right. It's more than the baby, though the baby is part of it. Most of all, though, it's you. All of you—from that laugh you have that sounds like bells to that brain that constantly amazes me."

She chuckled then. "You like my amazing brain, do you?"

"Oh, yeah. I like it. I like everything about you. You're beautiful and you're smart and all I want is you in my arms. I want you to be there, across the breakfast table from me. And next to me in our bed at night. For the rest of our lives."

"Oh, Tanner…" She felt the tears rising, pressing at the back of her throat. She swallowed them down.

He lifted the sport coat from the back of the chair long enough to take a small, square, black velvet box from an inner pocket. Then he put the coat back down and deftly flicked the box open with his thumb. The diamond within sparkled at her. "Marry me, Crystal. Be my wife."

Her *yes* was there, bubbling up within her. Her heart, her mind, her whole being wanted nothing so much as to say the word, to take his ring on her finger, to join her life to his.

Only she couldn't.

Not yet.

Not until the last shadow of the past was cast into the light.

She cleared her throat. "Oh, Tanner…"

"My God." He looked like she'd punched him hard in the stomach. "You're going to say no…."

Was she doing this badly? Oh, yeah. She should have spoken up before he brought out that beautiful ring, before he said all those amazing things about her. "I…no. I'm not saying no."

Joy blazed in his eyes. "Yes, then?"

"I…there's something I have to tell you first. Something I should have told you before, on that night when you asked me about my parents, about my childhood, about my past. Or one of the other times, when you encouraged me to say what was bothering me and somehow I never quite managed to do that."

"Crys—"

"No. Wait. Please. Come over here. Sit down." She led him to the sofa and put her hands on his broad shoulders.

"Listen," He tried to argue as she gently urged him down. "Really. This isn't necess—"

"Tanner." She backed away. She needed the distance. Desperately. "It *is* necessary. I have to say this. I need to tell you…." She stared at him, pleading with her eyes for him to understand.

He nodded. He set the box with the ring in it on the coffee table in front of him. "It doesn't matter. Believe me. There's nothing you could say that would make any difference to me."

"Maybe not. But, well, it does make a big difference to me. It's something I…I've never told anyone, since I got out on my own. It's something that breaks my heart every day, something I have to live with for the rest of my life."

He started to rise. "You don't have to—"

She put out a hand. "Please. Stay there. Let me say it. Don't…protect me. Not now. Let me tell you what I need you to know."

He sank back to the cushions. "All right." And he waited.

She made herself get down to it. "I told you I made a lot of trouble—got *in* a lot of trouble—when I was in my teens. There were drugs. And the kids I hung around with, we were all big drinkers. I was arrested twice— once for disturbing the peace and once for shoplifting. This all happened before I was fifteen."

Tanner shook his head. "It doesn't matter what happened then. You worked through it. You came out fine."

His acceptance made it a little easier for her to go on. "There's more," she said. "The day after my fifteenth birthday, a new boy came to my school. He took the desk next to mine in homeroom. The minute I saw him…I don't know. I'd fooled around a little with other boys. Kissing, and more. But I'd always had this idea that I just didn't need *that* kind of complication. I was wild and I was trouble, but I wasn't into making a fool of myself over some guy. I was too tough for that." A low, sad laugh escaped her. She shook her head. "Or so I thought." She wrapped her arms around herself and sank to the arm of an easy chair. "But then there was Damon. He was a rich boy and he was so smooth. All the girls were after him, but he liked *me*. And suddenly, it didn't seem like such a bad idea—love, and being together. Holding hands. Kissing. And more. My parents were always mad at me. I was constantly grounded. So I would sneak out to be with him. Within a month, we were lovers. I was sure it was forever, that we would get married, have a family, live in a bright house full of happiness and light. But then I got pregnant...."

She stared down at the hardwood floor between her high-heeled sandals and couldn't quite bring herself to lift her gaze and look at the man on the sofa across from her. Her throat ached. She coughed to loosen it.

Tanner said, "Tell me you're not ashamed. There's nothing for you to be ashamed about."

She dragged her gaze up and met his eyes. "I'm not ashamed. I'm...I'm just trying to tell you, okay? I just need for you to know."

"Okay." He said it so gently.

"Damon...dumped me. I told him about the baby, and he said he wanted nothing do with any damn kid. He had three hundred dollars in his pocket. He handed it over and said that was the best he could do. I should get an abortion. And the two of us were through. And if I wanted trouble, I should just *try* telling everyone I was having his kid. It was so ridiculous. The guy was breaking my heart, and he thought I would *tell* people what I'd let him do to me? For two weeks, we didn't speak. I wouldn't look at him or talk to him—and he returned the favor. I told myself that I hated him but soon he'd come crawling back to me, begging me to marry him and give our baby his name. Then maybe—just maybe—I'd forgive him.

"But then one night he went out with some buddies. They were drinking. There were drugs, I think. They busted through a guardrail on Highway 80. All three of them were killed. I went home and locked myself in my room and refused to come out for three days. After that, I moved through life on autopilot. I went to school, went home, got up in the morning and went to school again. My parents figured out I was pregnant in my sixth month when there was no hiding it anymore. They demanded to know who the father was. I lied and said I didn't know. I said there had been so many boys, I couldn't be sure which one to blame. That was when they started in on me to give the baby away. And, looking back, I think I was in some kind of serious clinical depression. Once or twice I lurched to life and tried to tell them I wanted to keep my baby. But they knew what was right. They knew what I needed to do.

"In the end, when the baby was born, they got me to sign the papers and they took the baby away. I still can't believe I let that happen, let them make the choice for me, but I did. Within a month of giving up my little girl, I was fighting with them constantly, demanding that they tell me where my baby was, that they let me see her, let me have a chance with her."

Crystal was looking at the floor again. Somehow, she couldn't look up. Not until she was finished, until she'd told it all.

"For four months after I signed my baby away, I begged them, pleaded with them constantly to tell me where my baby was. They turned away from me—they told me nothing. I even went to see Damon's parents, to tell them they had a grandchild, hoping they might help me. They wanted nothing to do with me or my baby. Their older son showed me the door. Finally, I got in that last fight with my father and walked out. For good…"

She told the rest quickly. "You pretty much know what happened next. I remade myself, got my GED, went to college for a couple of years. I'm healthy and drug-free, self-supporting. And in charge of my own destiny." She glanced up. His eyes were waiting. She couldn't hold steady. She looked down again. "And now there's you, Tanner. You're everything I once imagined poor Damon was. I'm so glad I have you." She put her hand on her newly rounded tummy. "And our baby. Life is good now, you know?"

"Yeah," he said low. "I know…."

"But I do…think of my lost baby. Often. I wonder…if she's okay. I pray that she's happy. It's not that I want to get her back. I don't, not if she's happy. If she's with a loving family, I can let her go. But I think I do need to know, I need to be sure she's okay. I'm…stronger now than I used to be. And I'm past the point of telling myself I can just move on. Not without being sure she's in a good place. I keep thinking that someday I'll go see my parents. I'll beg them again to tell me what happened to her."

Across the room, Tanner was silent.

And she felt lighter, suddenly. Which made total sense, didn't it? A pressing weight had been lifted. She wasn't carrying around her sad, lonely secret anymore.

She stood. "Now I've told you, I can't figure out why it was so hard to do." She felt her smile bloom wide, and she took a step toward him.

"Crystal," he whispered.

And at last, she looked straight into his eyes.

He said, rough and low, "Crystal, I'm sorry...."

She didn't understand. "I...what?"

"I knew. I knew already. About your daughter."

She gaped at him. "You knew? But how could you...?" And right then, she got it. Right then, she understood what he'd done. "Oh, no..." Her lips barely formed the words.

He rose. "Crystal. Listen..."

She shook her head. Slowly. "You've been...investigating, haven't you? You've been investigating *me*..."

"Listen..." He dared to take a step toward her.

"Stop," she commanded, putting out a hand. "Stop right there. And answer my question. Tell me you haven't. Tell me you didn't."

"I can't tell you that."

"Because you did."

"Don't..." His dark eyes pleaded with her. "Don't look at me like that. You have to know I'd never do anything to hurt you."

"Tell me the truth. Just do it. Tell me if you went behind my back. If you found out the things I wasn't ready to tell you yet."

"Crystal, I only wanted to help you...." He stepped toward her again.

She backed away, put the chair between them. "No, Tanner. No. You tell me. You tell the truth now."

He stared at her. And then, at last, he admitted, "Fine.

All right. Yes. I've met with your mother. I know about the child you had. I've—"

"Enough." The word echoed in her head. *Enough.* Oh, no. It was way more than enough. It was too much. She'd wanted him to tell her what he'd done—but now she couldn't bear to hear another word. She spoke in a small, disbelieving voice. "You had no right. You could have waited. I would have told you. I just did. You could have trusted me to tell you. You could have respected my right to tell you when I was ready."

"I swear, I thought I would help you."

"Help me." She gaped at him. "By betraying my trust in you? How, exactly, was that going to help me?" She looked down at her hands. They were gripping the soft leather back of the chair, her nails digging in. She stared down at those clutching hands and she wondered—at herself, at the hurt and horror blooming dark and ugly within her.

He wasn't judging her; she knew that. He didn't *blame* her for deserting her own child. Somewhere deep down, she even knew that he would never do anything to harm her, that he only wanted to do what he could for her.

But it was too much. That he'd known—for how long? Days? Weeks? He'd known the secret she couldn't bring herself to tell him. While she stewed and worried and tried to work up the nerve to get the hardest words out, he'd known the whole time....

He said, "I knew you were hiding something, and I knew it was eating at you. So I contacted your mother and got her to agree to meet with me."

"When?" She barely managed to give the word sound.

"What?"

"When did you meet with my mother?"

"About a month ago. The night of the day DeDe ran away."

"That *client,* right? The one you said you just had to meet with, which was why you barely made it back in time for the call to Kelly and Mitch. That *client* was my mother?"

"Crystal—"

"Answer me. You lied to me. Just say it. Say it out loud."

"All right. Yeah. I lied to you. I wasn't meeting with a client that night. I met with your mother. I'd already tried to set up the appointment with her and she'd put me off. And then she called just before I was heading back to you at Kelly's. She said she was willing to meet with me right away."

"So you agreed. You called me and lied to me and said you were working. And what you were really doing was going behind my back to talk to my mother."

"Look. I thought it was for the best, to talk to her, to find out what I could from her."

Had he really said that? "The best? The *best?*"

"Yeah. And I was afraid to put her off, afraid she'd back out if I gave her time to reconsider. I let her think you had hired me to talk to her. She became agitated. And she just…let it slip about the child. And after that, after I learned about the little girl, I started thinking that you were *afraid* to know. Afraid to make a move, to find out what had happened, to find out where your daughter is and if she's doing well…or not. I thought if I could find her for you—"

"No. " She pressed her hands to her ears, knowing she was behaving like a child herself and yet, somehow, unable to do otherwise. "No, no, no…" She'd left her bag on the end of the counter. She whirled, raced over there and grabbed it. "I'm going back to my place now. I'll come tomorrow, after you're gone for the day, and get my things."

"Damn it, Crys. Don't do this. Don't run away."

She turned and headed for the door to the garage. He called her name twice. She didn't pause; she refused to look back. She went out the door and got in her car and left his house.

The drive to her place was a nightmare. The streets were dark and cars rushed by on either side of her, and she knew she was out of control, knew the last place she ought to be right then was behind the wheel of a car.

Still, somehow, she kept the car moving forward. She managed, by some miracle, not to get in a wreck.

At her apartment, she turned on all the lights and sat on the futon in the living room and rocked herself.

Like a baby.

Like a sad, scared lost child.

Chapter Fifteen

For Tanner, that night was right up there with the worst nights of his life.

It was like the nights of powerlessness when he was a small boy, when he'd lie in his bed in the group home and wonder when—and if—his mother would ever come back for him, wonder how the little baby was, the one his mother kept saying she didn't know anything about.

Oh, yeah. Right up there with the worst.

But then again…

Who was he kidding? It wasn't *up there* with the worst. It *was* the worst.

When Lia Wells Bravo left him in the system, he was blameless in his own suffering, a scared small boy worried for his lost little sister. Back then, he was innocent. There was nothing he could have done differently then, nothing that would have changed the way things went down.

In this, in Crystal running from him, he was far from innocent. She was right to blame him. Her story was hers to tell—in her own time and her own way. Her choice. He had ripped that choice away from her, just as her mother and father had taken her child. He'd taken her choice and told himself it was for her own good.

Tanner wasn't a guy who prayed much. But he prayed that night. He prayed that Crystal stayed safe. It was all he wanted, her safety through the endless night, and the safety of their baby.

All right. He wanted more. He wanted hope. He wanted another chance. If she'd only give him one— later. In time.

That night, though, he prayed only that she would stay safe until morning.

Sometime after 3:00 a.m., Crystal put on an old pair of pj's and fell into bed. She dropped off into a sleep of pure exhaustion.

When she woke, it was daylight. The sun streamed in parallel golden lines through the spaces between the blinds, and she rubbed her red-rimmed eyes, raked her tangled hair back from her face and squinted at the bedside clock.

7:05 a.m. And somebody was ringing her doorbell. *Tanner?*

She felt a truly disconcerting jolt of pure happiness—followed instantly by outrage. He had no right to come here when she'd made it so clear it was over between them.

She threw back the covers, yanked on her robe and stalked to the front door, throwing it wide without even bothering to check the peephole first, ready to tell him to get lost and stay lost.

It was Doris. The older woman gasped and fell back a step. "Crystal? Oh, my!"

Crystal drooped against the door, all the fight draining out of her. "Doris. Sorry. I didn't know it was you." She frowned. "Is Nigel missing?"

Doris shook her wild head of gray curls. "Oh, no. He's at home. Fatter than ever. Eating his morning bowl of Fancy Feast."

Crystal sighed. "Good. You had me worried there." She stepped back. "Come on in. I'll see if I've got any coffee around here."

Doris hesitated. "I just wanted to be sure you're okay. I heard you come home last night."

Crystal winced. "I slammed my door, didn't I?"

"It's all right. Really—and you know, tea would be so nice. If you have some?"

Crystal stepped back and ushered her in. "It just so happens, I do have tea. I'm sure about that."

She heated the water and got down mugs and tea bags, and they sat at the table.

Doris sipped. "I almost came over last night, when I heard you come in. I was concerned for you. I thought you were staying with that special guy of yours."

"Not anymore."

"Oh, no. Something went wrong between you, then?"

Doris looked so upset that Crystal knew she had to give her some kind of explanation. She started to tell her just a little—and somehow ended up telling it all. Even about the babies—the one she was going to have *and* the little girl she'd given up eight years ago.

How strange. Her deepest secret for so long, and now she found she *could* talk about it. It was as if after finally telling Tanner, the secret no longer had its old, awful power over her.

Doris was all sympathy and loving understanding. And not only for Crystal. After she got up and gave Crystal a hug, she went back to her chair. She took another thoughtful sip of her tea and set the mug back down with care. "Well, of course Tanner had no business going behind your back. Still, though, I think he meant well, that he only wanted to do what he could to help you."

Crystal lifted a shoulder in a half shrug. "Yeah. That's what he said. I'm sure it's true. But that hardly makes it right."

"No. No, of course it doesn't." Doris gave her a fond smile. "I'm sure you know…what you have to do."

"That's right. I do know."

"And didn't you mention you were working for him, too?"

"Yes, I am. Or, I was."

"So that's it, then? You're quitting as of today? You just…won't show up for work?"

The question gave Crystal pause. She hadn't thought beyond crawling back into bed as soon as Doris left and pulling the covers over her head.

But then again, maybe not. "Well. I do have my pride, after all."

Doris smiled sweetly. "Of course you do."

"I did walk out on my last job—for good reason."

"I remember you said that lawyer was a sleazeball."

"Oh, yes. He was."

"I can guess he finally crossed the line."

"He did. But, you know, the more I think about it, the more I have to admit that it's not a good idea to make a habit of walking out on jobs, no matter how valid the reason."

Doris bobbed her curly head. "So true."

"So it's just possible I ought to rethink my plan to spend the day in bed."

The last thing Tanner wanted to do that day was to go to the office. The thought of being there was every bit as bad as being at his house.

Crystal had put her mark on both places, which meant that going to the office would be a whole new kind of torture. Everywhere he looked, he'd think of her, thanks to the miracles she could work with a few potted ferns and a borrowed sewing machine.

But he had appointments there with first-time clients at ten and at eleven. He could lose business if he didn't show. And even if Crystal refused to give him another chance, he was still going to be a father to their baby. He would provide, damn it—and provide well.

Which meant never passing up an opportunity to build business.

So drove over there. He pulled into the parking lot— and spotted Crystal's Camaro, parked in its usual space.

He couldn't believe his eyes. She was here, after all?

He was out of the Mustang in a flash. He took the stairs to the second floor two at a time, his heart pounding so hard in his chest, the sound of it echoed in his ears.

The office door was unlocked. He pushed it wide and

there she was, behind the desk where he'd hardly dared to believe she could be.

She was on the phone. He approached, heart knocking so loud he knew she had to be able to hear it. She finished the call and said goodbye.

He stood there, waiting, like a total fool, as she typed a note on her computer. And then, at last, she looked at him—or rather, through him. "It's good you're here. You've got another appointment in fifteen minutes. That work for you?"

"Fine. Crystal, I…"

She slid a paper toward him. "My resignation," she said, brisk as a boot in the backside. "Two weeks. We should start interviewing my replacement."

He didn't know what he felt—maybe hope that she would be there for fourteen more days. Maybe despair that after that she'd be gone. At least his heart had stopped trying to leap out of his throat.

"No replacement," he said gruffly. "If you're leaving, I'll go it alone, same as I always have."

She frowned. "Well, then, if you can get along without me, I might as well just—"

He didn't let her finish. "Two weeks. It's fair. I'll…take you for as long as I can get you."

She glanced away. "All right, then."

He considered reminding her that, no matter what, he still intended to be a father to his child. But he held the words back. He had a feeling she knew that. If he said them now, they would only come out sounding like a threat.

"Messages?" he asked.

"I put them on your desk."

"Great." He turned and went through the door to his private office.

Crystal watched him go. The door clicked shut behind him. *Two weeks,* she thought, and wondered how she would bear it.

She longed to jump up, knock on the door he'd just quietly closed on her—and throw herself into his big, strong arms. She yearned to burst into tears and swear that she loved him, in spite of what he'd done. That she would always love him, that he was the only man for her.

But she did nothing of the kind. She turned back to her computer and got on with her workday.

She met Kelly for lunch and told her everything.

Kelly listened and made no judgments and didn't try to tell her what to do. But when they left the restaurant, she did ask if it was all right to tell Mitch.

Crystal grabbed her and hugged her hard. "Yeah. You can tell him. All of it, if you need to. It's okay."

Mitch showed up on Crystal's doorstep that evening. She ushered him in and they talked for an hour. He offered her money, as he always did.

She told him she loved him and she would be fine.

"Tanner and I have had our differences," Mitch said as he was leaving. "But I completely get why he did what he did."

That made Crystal laugh. "You men. You always know what's best for the rest of us."

Mitch took her by the shoulders. "Look at you," he said. "All these years, you couldn't bring yourself to talk about the little girl you lost. You kept the secret from everyone, all the people who care about you. Tanner blew that secret wide-open. Maybe he had no right to do it. But you have to admit, it needed doing."

"Mitch," she replied with considerable patience. "He didn't blow anything open. I *told* him my secret—and then he confessed that he already knew about it."

"He did it for you, Crys."

"Mitch."

"You're mad at me now...."

"No, I'm not mad. I love you and I know you mean only the best for me."

"But you want me to butt out of it."

"That's right. Butt out."

The next day Crystal worked for an hour before Tanner arrived. When he finally showed up, she wanted to grab him and kiss him silly. She wanted to yell and throw things and accuse him of wrecking everything with his so-manly need to solve all her problems, whether she wanted help solving them or not.

What she actually did was to continue typing the letter she had up on her computer screen.

He strolled over to her desk, looking dark and dangerous and too disgustingly hot for words—and plunked down a manila envelope.

She stopped typing long enough to give it a glance. "And that is?"

"Your file. The one I worked up on you and your child and your family, without your permission. I had most of it on my computer at the house, but I printed it all up and put it in there. I also saved it to Memory Stick—also in there. That's everything. And it's all yours now. I blew it up on my computer."

She knew she should say something cool and non-committal, but words had deserted her. And her hands were shaking. She put them in her lap, folded them tightly and swallowed to clear her clutching throat. "Thank you."

He said, so quietly, "You know I'd do anything for you. Anything." And then he left her. He went into his office and closed the door.

His words echoed in her ears, burning, making the tears rise so she had to gulp them down. She stared at that envelope for a good ninety seconds, before she scooped it up and stuck it in the tote beside her desk.

At her apartment that night, she emptied the envelope's contents onto the table. She set the Memory Stick aside and read the stack of papers all the way through.

When she was finished, she sat there for a long time, staring at the far wall, wondering what to do next. Finally, she picked up the phone and dialed her parents' number.

When she finished that call, she called Tanner and asked him if she could have the next morning off. He didn't ask why—just told her that was fine with him.

"See you after lunch, then," she said.

"Sounds good." And he was gone.

She clutched the phone and wished he was still on the line—wished she could reach out and he would be there.

The irony was, he *would* be there. All she had to do was say the word.

Something held her back from that. Something inside her was locked up tight.

* * *

The house on the cul-de-sac in Roseville was just as she had remembered it. Set back from the street on a large lot. Two stories, painted gray.

All the curtains were drawn across the windows. Her mother always said the sun was dangerous. It would fade the furniture. Crystal used to shake her head at that one. Her mother favored neutrals—tans and grays and off-whites. Who cared if off-white faded?

Crystal parked her car in the driveway and went up the front walk on legs that felt rubbery, almost numb. The wide front door had a No Soliciting sign on it, as it always had.

Crystal rang the bell. And waited.

Beyond the door, there was silence. And then, faintly, she heard footsteps approaching.

The door swung open. Her mother stood there—grayer, a few pounds heavier. Sadder, somehow.

"Martha," she said softly.

Crystal bit down hard on her bottom lip. The pain pushed the sudden tears away. "My name is Crystal now."

"Crystal." Her mother's mouth trembled. She stepped back and gestured into the shadows of the too-quiet house. "Please. Come in. Your father is waiting…." She turned and led the way.

Crystal fell in behind her, down the central hall to the master suite at the back of the house. The door was open on near-darkness. One lamp glowed within.

Her mother went through and Crystal followed. The room was greatly changed. A nurse in a blue smock top and white pants and duty shoes came out of the master bath. She, at least, had a smile.

The four-poster bed Crystal remembered from her childhood was gone, replaced by the kind of bed they have in hospitals, with steel railings and mechanisms for raising and lowering the patient's various body parts.

There was an oxygen tank and a drip bag of some clear liquid on a stand. And a hospital tray with an endless array of orange prescription bottles. On the bed lay a frail old man—hollow-cheeked, his skin gray and sagging. He had haunted eyes.

He reached out his claw of a hand to her and in a voice that barely rose above a strangled whisper, he asked, "Martha?"

She didn't correct him. This man was far past correcting. "Yes." She took his hand. All bone. So brittle. "Hello, Dad."

He looked at her through eyes sunk deep in shadowed sockets and he said, his ragged whisper turned pleading, "Martha. Forgive. Forgive me, please...."

Crystal left that dark house an hour later. She hugged her mother at the door.

Her mother pressed a paper into her hand. "The Thornwood Adoption Agency," she whispered. Crystal already knew the name. It was in the file that Tanner had given her.

"Thank you," she said. "Call me if he gets worse...."

"I will," said her mother.

"I'll come back in a few days, in any case."

"Oh, good. That's good. I was...rude and self-righteous to that detective you hired...."

"Tanner, you mean?" Crystal almost said that she hadn't hired him. But it hardly mattered now.

Her mother was nodding. "Then, after I got home that night, I cried. I did so want to see you, though my pride wouldn't let me admit it to a young man I didn't even know. I thought I had ruined my chance to ever make peace with you, to ever see you again. And then I went in to speak with your father and he took my hand. He whispered of you, of how hard we had been on you, of how he only dreamed of one more chance with you...." Tears brimmed. Her mother swiped them away. "Oh, I didn't mean to cry now. Lately, it seems, the tears come so easily."

Crystal grabbed her close and hugged her again. Harder than the first time. "It's okay. It's...good. Honestly. I...I love you, Mom." The words sounded strange coming out of her mouth. But she was glad she had said them.

"Oh, Martha. I love you, too."

Who knew? Crystal thought as she drove back to the Central Valley. Her parents had actually been happy to see her. She felt a tear slide down her cheek. She should have gone sooner. But at least she'd finally made the first step toward reconciliation with them.

She caught herself thinking how she couldn't wait to tell Tanner. And then she started wondering how long she could go on like this.

Yearning for him.

But somehow unable to make a move. Unable to forgive.

The office was empty. He'd taped a note to her computer.

Gone to Nuevo Laredo. Got a lead on the where-abouts of Eli Dunning. Back soon. With Dunning, I hope. To be on the safe side, reschedule my appointments through Monday. If they can't wait, call Gruber or Saint to cover.

Dan Gruber and Melvin Saint were associates of Tanner's—and Eli Dunning was the rat who had bilked senior citizens. If Tanner was going to catch him, that was all to the good.

But Nuevo Laredo? Wasn't that in Mexico? And when, specifically, would he be back?

By Monday, right? Or at least, by Tuesday morning. Four or five days. Not a long time. Nothing she couldn't handle.

She was tempted to try his cell, just to see if she could reach him, to make sure he was fine and everything was going well. Somehow, she restrained herself. Since she'd walked out on him, she'd given up the right to call him just to hear his voice and see how he was doing.

Which reminded her—she'd yet to go to his place, to collect her stuff and leave the key. While he was gone would be a good opportunity to take care of that.

But that evening after work, she just didn't feel up to it. Doris came over and they ordered takeout. Friday morning Kelly called and invited her to dinner. Crystal gratefully accepted. When she got there, DeDe ran to greet her, wrapping her arms around her and hugging her tight.

"Crystal, come on." She grabbed Crystal's hand and towed her down the hall to her room, where she had her iPod on the Speaker Dock, loaded up with the latest Ally and AJ song. "You're gonna love this one. It's even better than 'Potential Break-up Song.'"

At dinner, Mitch asked how Tanner was doing down in Mexico.

Crystal sent him a sharp glance. "So you know about that trip, huh?"

Mitch put up both hands, as if she'd pointed a gun at him. "Hey. He called and told Kelly he was going. Is that okay with you?"

"Of course it's okay." She tried to make her voice gentler. "And I don't know how he's doing. I haven't spoken to him."

DeDe darted glances from one adult to the other. "Are you guys mad or something?"

Crystal gave her a big smile. "No. We're not. We're not mad in the least."

Saturday, she didn't have to go to the office. It was the perfect opportunity to get her stuff from Tanner's house.

Excuses instantly popped into her head—about a hundred of them at once. A hundred stupid reasons why she didn't need to go to Tanner's house and get all the things she'd left there.

Four days since she'd walked out on him. She'd been using her spare hair dryer and random makeup she had left at the apartment. It was a pain to try to cook without her favorite pots and her best paring knife. The clothes she'd left at his house she didn't miss all that much. She was getting too fat for most of them, anyway.

But her accessories—her best bags, her favorite shoes. She did miss them and they were all at his place.

Plus, she had no right to leave all her stuff with him, cluttering up his living space. It wasn't fair.

So she got her keys, grabbed her purse, got in her car and drove over there. She still had his garage door opener clipped to the sunshade above the steering wheel, so she backed into the garage and went in through the utility room. Instantly the alarm started blaring.

Of course. He would have left it armed, since he was going to be gone for a while….

A quick punch of the code, and the house fell blessedly silent. Too silent.

She went into the kitchen, which was spotless. Almost *too* clean, as if no one really lived there. She opened a cabinet and saw two of her frying pans—and shut it without taking them.

In the living area, she found one bowl with a spoon in it, on the side table by the easy chair where he liked to sit when he watched TV. She scooped up the bowl and carried it into the kitchen. She rinsed it and the spoon and put them in the dishwasher.

And then she just stood there, by the sink. She was crying, for some crazy reason—crying silently. No sobs, no sniffles. The tears streamed down her cheeks, and she stared around at the kitchen and wondered how she would bear this. How she would live.

Without her love. Without Tanner…

She drew in a long, shuddering breath and made herself start walking. Through the empty rooms to the master suite.

It was as painfully tidy as the rest of the house. Except for the bed. He'd left it unmade. The covers were all tangled. One pillow was on the floor: hers. She dropped to the bed and grabbed the other pillow and buried her face in it.

The scent of him was in it, tempting her. Breaking her heart all over again.

She tossed the pillow hard against the headboard and got up and went to the closet. All her things were there, shoes on racks, skirts and shirts neatly arrayed on hangers, just as she'd left them, waiting for her to come get them.

Or to come home.

She backed up, her hand to her mouth, the wetness smearing on her cheeks. She sat on the bed again.

And then she kicked off her shoes and grabbed his pillow once more. She curled up on her side and laid her head down where his had been, closing her eyes with a surrendering sigh.

"Home," she whispered to the empty room, her head on his pillow, her body curled protectively around the new life within her. "Home…"

Tanner flew back to Sacramento on a red-eye flight that left Laredo, Texas, at one o'clock Sunday morning. He had Eli Dunning in the seat next to him. They changed planes in Dallas. He'd called ahead and a couple of obliging plainclothes detectives met him at Sacramento International. He turned Dunning over to face arrest and arraignment.

The Mustang was waiting in the long-term lot. He tossed his duffel in the back and slid in behind the wheel, his hand automatically going for his cell, his fingers itching to call Crystal.

Some habits were hard to break. He pulled his hand away from the phone—carefully, as from a weapon. He slipped his key from his pocket and stuck it in the ignition. The car turned over and he put it in gear.

If she wanted to talk to you, she would call you, he reminded himself for the hundredth time as he drove home.

He was starting to think the worst. That she was never going to call. That she would finish out her final two weeks working for him and that would be that.

Until the baby was born, anyway, and she had to deal with him for the sake of their child.

He had to constantly remind himself that it had been only a few days since she walked out. That he needed to give her time. That she loved him as he loved her and eventually she would forgive him.

But every day was a century. Five days gone now since she left. It wasn't that long, he tried to remind himself.

It only *felt* like a lifetime.

He turned onto his street, dread crawling within him. He hated to do it, to face his empty, lonely house. It would be funny if it wasn't so pitiful. He'd owned the house for years and never felt lonely in it.

Until Crystal left him. Now every room echoed with emptiness.

The morning sun was a slit of orange light on the horizon as he nosed the car into the driveway and pushed the garage remote. The door rumbled up, revealing the one thing he'd never expected to see there: Crystal's red Camaro.

His heart slammed against his ribcage. Impossible. It couldn't be.

Crystal.

Home.

Crystal didn't know what woke her.

But from a sound sleep, she found herself swimming upward toward waking. She stirred, hugged the pillow and opened one eye.

Tanner was sitting in the chair in the corner.

No. Couldn't be. He wasn't due home till tomorrow, at least. She must be dreaming.

She lifted her head, braced herself on an elbow and blinked several times. He was still sitting there.

She whispered, "Tanner?"

That was when he stood up and came toward her.

"Oh, Tanner." She reached out her arms to him with a cry. And then he was there with her, gathering her in.

He kissed her. It wasn't possible that his kiss could be sweeter than before. But it was. Oh, it was.

He stroked her hair and she snuggled against him, holding on so tight, breathing in through her nose, drawing the scent of him into her.

"You're home," he whispered, and he pressed kisses against her hair.

"Yes, oh yes. I am. I'm home...."

He tipped up her chin and he claimed her lips again, kissing her so hard and so deep she felt faint with the wonder of it.

That time, when he lifted his head, he said, "I was so afraid. I thought you'd never come back to me, never forgive me."

And she laughed then and stroked his beard-stubbled cheek. "If I can forgive my father, I can certainly forgive you."

"You did it, then?" His dark eyes shone with wonder. "You went to see your folks?"

"I did. My father is so sick. I'm so glad I went at last. I'll go again, tomorrow. Maybe…you'll come with me?"

"You know I will. If you want me with you, I'm there."

"And my mother, she was…so different. She said she'd been rude and self-righteous to you—she said that." Crystal laughed again. By then, she was laughing through happy tears. "Her very words. And she gave me the name and address of the agency, the one that placed my daughter—which I already had, of course, in the file you worked up for me. But I didn't tell her that. I thanked her. I hugged her so hard."

"Good." He kissed her wet cheeks, one and then the other. "Family is everything. We have to do what we can for them."

"I know. Oh, Tanner. You are so right. And I…I didn't like what you did. But, well, Mitch said that maybe it needed doing. And the more I think about it, the more I understand why you did it. I know that you did it for me, and I…well, I want to let it go now. I want to move on with our lives, together. If that's all right with you?"

"If it's all right? Crys. You have to know it's a hell of a lot more than all right. It's everything to me."

She framed his face between her hands. "Oh, I'm so glad. I've been waiting here since yesterday, when I told myself I was coming here to get my things. I walked in this house and I knew I was home, and the thought that I could live my life without you—that was pure foolishness. A total lie. I love you with all my heart. And all I want is to spend the rest of my life at your side."

He clasped her hands between both of his. "Wait right there."

"Oh, Tanner…"

He rose and he went to his dresser and opened the top drawer. He took something out, and when he turned back to her, she saw what it was.

"Oh, come here. Right this minute." She stretched out her arms again. "Come back here to me."

He didn't hesitate. He sat on the edge of the bed, and he took that diamond ring out of its velvet box.

"I love you. You're the only woman in the world for me. Marry me," he whispered.

"Oh, Tanner. Yes. A thousand times, yes."

The ring fit perfectly. The bright stone gleamed. She lifted her face to him and he kissed her. A kiss of love and tenderness.

Crystal knew for certain, then. It was going to be all right. She and Tanner would marry. They would be a family.

Somehow, against all the odds, the lost girl who ran away all those years ago had grown up to become a loving woman. She'd been a long time getting here.

But she was home at last, in Tanner's loving arms.

Epilogue

Tanner wrapped an arm around his wife's slender shoulders.

Crystal took his free hand and put it on the enormous swell of her belly. "Feel that?" Her shining eyes met his.

"Oh, yeah. That was a fist, I think."

"Uh-uh, a foot…"

They walked on through the park, under trees on fire with fall color. As they approached the meeting place by the duck pond, she hung back.

He tipped her sweet face up with a finger. "You want me to go with you?"

She swallowed, shook her head. "Not this first time. Wait here for me?" She glanced up at the bright canopy of leaves over their head. "Under this gorgeous maple tree…"

"I'll be here."

She stood on tiptoe to kiss him.

Reluctantly, he released her, dropping his sheltering arm to his side. She moved forward. He stuck his hands in his pockets and watched her go.

A hundred yards away, on a sunny patch of grass, a smiling couple stood with a blond-haired child, a beautiful little girl not much younger than DeDe. The girl clung to her parents.

Her father bent close and whispered something to her. She nodded. And then, shyly, she stepped forward to meet the woman who had given her life.

* * * * *

*Here's a sneak peek at THE CEO'S CHRISTMAS
PROPOSITION, the first in USA TODAY bestselling
author Merline Lovelace's HOLIDAYS ABROAD
trilogy coming in November 2008.*

American Devon McShay is about to get the
Christmas surprise of a lifetime when she meets
her new client, sexy billionaire Caleb Logan, for
the very first time.

Silhouette
Desire

Available November 2008

Her breath whistled out in a sigh of relief when he exited Customs. Devon recognized him right away from the newspaper and magazine articles her friend and partner Sabrina had looked up during her frantic prep work.

Caleb John Logan, Jr. Thirty-one. Six-two. With jet-black hair, laser-blue eyes and a linebacker's shoulders under his charcoal-gray cashmere overcoat. His jaw-dropping good looks didn't score him any points with Devon. She'd learned the hard way not to trust handsome heartbreakers like Cal Logan.

But he was a client. An important one. And she was willing to give someone who'd served a hitch in the marines before earning a B.S. from the University of Oregon, an MBA from Stanford and his first million at the ripe old age of twenty-six the benefit of the doubt.

Right up until he spotted the hot-pink pashmina, that is.

Devon knew the flash of color was more visible than the sign she held up with his name on it. So she wasn't surprised when Logan picked her out of the crowd and cut in her direction. She'd just plastered on her best businesswoman smile when he whipped an arm around her waist. The next moment she was sprawled against his cashmere-covered chest.

"Hello, brown eyes."

Swooping down, he covered her mouth with his.

Sheer astonishment kept Devon rooted to the spot for a few seconds while her mind whirled chaotically. Her first thought was that her client had downed a few too many drinks during the long flight. Her second, that he'd mistaken the kind of escort and consulting services her company provided. Her third shoved everything else out of her head.

The man could kiss!

His mouth moved over hers with a skill that ignited sparks at a half dozen flash points throughout her body. Devon hadn't experienced that kind of spontaneous combustion in a while. A *long* while.

The sparks were still popping when she pushed off his chest, only now they fueled a flush of anger.

"Do you always greet women you don't know with a lip-lock, Mr. Logan?"

A smile crinkled the skin at the corners of his eyes. "As a matter of fact, I don't. That was from Don."

"Huh?"

"He said he owed you one from New Year's Eve two years ago and made me promise to deliver it."

She stared up at him in total incomprehension. Logan hooked a brow and attempted to prompt a non-existent memory.

"He abandoned you at the Waldorf. Five minutes before midnight. To deliver twins."

"I don't have a clue who or what you're…"

Understanding burst like a water balloon.

"Wait a sec. Are you talking about Sabrina's old boy-friend? Your buddy, who's now an ob-gyn doc?"

It was Logan's turn to look startled. He recovered faster than Devon had, though. His smile widened into a rueful grin.

"I take it you're not Sabrina Russo."

"No, Mr. Logan, I am *not*."

* * * * *

Be sure to look for
THE CEO'S CHRISTMAS PROPOSITION
by Merline Lovelace.
Available in November 2008 wherever books are sold, including most bookstores, supermarkets, drugstores and discount stores.

MERLINE LOVELACE

THE CEO'S CHRISTMAS PROPOSITION

After being stranded in Austria together
at Christmas, it takes only one kiss for
aerospace CEO Cal Logan to decide he wants
more than just a business relationship with
Devon McShay. But when Cal's credibility is
questioned, he has to fight to clear his name,
and to get Devon to trust her heart.

**Available November
wherever books are sold.**

Holidays Abroad

Always Powerful, Passionate and Provocative.

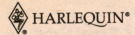

HARLEQUIN®

American ★ Romance®

HOLLY JACOBS
Once Upon a Christmas

Daniel McLean is thrilled to learn he
may be the father of Michelle Hamilton's
nephew. When Daniel starts to spend
time with Brandon and help her organize
Erie Elementary's big Christmas Fair, the
three discover a paternity test won't make
them a family, but the love they discover
just might....

Available December 2008
wherever books are sold.

LOVE, HOME & HAPPINESS

MARRIED BY CHRISTMAS

Playboy billionaire Elijah Vanaldi has discovered
he is guardian to his small orphaned nephew.
But his reputation makes some people question
his ability to be a father. He knows he must
fight to protect the child, and he'll do anything
it takes. Ainslie Farrell is jobless, homeless and
desperate—and when Elijah offers her a position
in his household she simply can't refuse....

Available in November

HIRED: THE ITALIAN'S CONVENIENT MISTRESS

by

CAROL MARINELLI

Book #29

HPE82375

Silhouette®

Romantic
SUSPENSE

**Sparked by Danger,
Fueled by Passion.**

Lindsay McKenna
Susan Grant

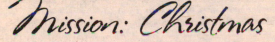
Mission: Christmas

Celebrate the holidays with a pair
of military heroines and their daring men
in two romantic, adventurous stories
from these bestselling authors.

Featuring:

"The Christmas Wild Bunch"
by *USA TODAY* bestselling author
Lindsay McKenna
and
"Snowbound with a Prince"
by *New York Times* bestselling author
Susan Grant

Available November wherever books are sold.

REQUEST YOUR FREE BOOKS!

2 FREE NOVELS PLUS 2 FREE GIFTS!

Silhouette®

SPECIAL EDITION®

Life, Love and Family!

YES! Please send me 2 FREE Silhouette Special Edition® novels and my 2 FREE gifts (gifts are worth about $10). After receiving them, if I don't wish to receive any more books, I can return the shipping statement marked "cancel." If I don't cancel, I will receive 6 brand-new novels every month and be billed just $4.24 per book in the U.S. or $4.99 per book in Canada, plus 25¢ shipping and handling per book and applicable taxes, if any*. That's a savings of at least 15% off the cover price! I understand that accepting the 2 free books and gifts places me under no obligation to buy anything. I can always return a shipment and cancel at any time. Even if I never buy another book from Silhouette, the two free books and gifts are mine to keep forever.

235 SDN EEYU   335 SDN EEY6

Name	(PLEASE PRINT)
Address	Apt. #
City	State/Prov.	Zip/Postal Code

Signature (if under 18, a parent or guardian must sign)

Mail to the Silhouette Reader Service:
IN U.S.A.: P.O. Box 1867, Buffalo, NY 14240-1867
IN CANADA: P.O. Box 609, Fort Erie, Ontario L2A 5X3

Not valid to current subscribers of Silhouette Special Edition books.

Want to try two free books from another line?
Call 1-800-873-8635 or visit www.morefreebooks.com.

* Terms and prices subject to change without notice. N.Y. residents add applicable sales tax. Canadian residents will be charged applicable provincial taxes and GST. Offer not valid in Quebec. This offer is limited to one order per household. All orders subject to approval. Credit or debit balances in a customer's account(s) may be offset by any other outstanding balance owed by or to the customer. Please allow 4 to 6 weeks for delivery. Offer available while quantities last.

Your Privacy: Silhouette is committed to protecting your privacy. Our Privacy Policy is available online at www.eHarlequin.com or upon request from the Reader Service. From time to time we make our lists of customers available to reputable third parties who may have a product or service of interest to you. If you would prefer we not share your name and address, please check here. ☐

SSE08R

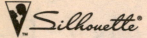
Silhouette®

COMING NEXT MONTH